BITTER JUSTICE

THE COWBOY JUSTICE ASSOCIATION
BOOK TWELVE

by Olivia James

www.OliviaJaymes.com

CHAPTER ONE

Tanner Marks rolled over and turned off the morning alarm so it wouldn't wake his wife Maddie later. There was still thirty minutes to sleep and he didn't want to disturb her. As hard as she worked, she deserved every second of rest that she could get.

Not that he didn't work hard, too. He did. But after years in the Army, two kids both with colic, working crappy shifts as a deputy, and then running a sheriff's office he was used to getting less sleep than he ideally needed. His daughter Amanda had been a revelation of sorts – she was a good sleeper. He hadn't even known babies like that existed until he'd had one of his own. He'd thought they were simply an urban legend, one that kept parents hopeful.

Rising slowly out of bed, he stretched and silently groaned as his back popped and his knee creaked. At his age, different body parts woke up when they damn well felt like it and not a second before. Last week he'd chased a shoplifter out of a store and down two blocks before he'd caught up, making his previously broken ankle scream with pain. Ten years ago, the guy wouldn't have made it out of the front doors, but he was slowing down.

At least once a week, he said that he was too damn old for this shit.

He slipped downstairs and through the dark house, pausing for a moment at Amanda's door. It was halfway open and he could see her peacefully sleeping, her red-gold curls like an angel's halo around her head. Looks could be deceiving, however. In about forty-five minutes she was going to be wide awake and demanding Cheerios.

But for a short while this morning, Tanner would have the house to himself. Peace and quiet. He liked to wake up before anyone else and have a few moments to gather his thoughts and enjoy a cup of coffee. It made heading into his crazy and chaotic days much easier.

Pouring himself a cup of java – the coffeemaker was on a timer – he sat down at the kitchen table and sipped at the piping hot brew, grunting as the heat slid down to his belly. He hadn't had a drink in years but no one was going to take his coffee away from him.

Rising from the table, he walked to the window over the sink and watched as the sun just peeked over the horizon. This had become a habit in the last several months. Awake early. Get coffee. Watch sunrise. Repeat.

Oh, and contemplate life. He did that quite a bit too, not that he was ready to admit that out loud. At fifty-five years old, he might be going through a mid-life crisis. But then it seemed a bit late for that as he didn't think he would live to be one hundred and ten. He took decent care of himself and his grandfather had lived to be ninety-three and was on his third wife when he'd passed, but a hundred and ten? A slim chance at best.

But he did spend these precious minutes thinking. About everything and nothing. He wasn't a man given to massive amounts of introspection but here he was… Introspecting the hell out of himself. Wondering about the fifty-five years he'd lived, contemplating about how many more he had, and just what he wanted to do with them.

He was *restless*.

That was the word he'd stumbled upon a few months ago. Nothing felt easy or casual anymore. It was as if he was wearing clothes that were ill-fitted or scratchy. He was uncomfortable and it made him grouchy, a fact he was desperately trying to hide from his beautiful, young wife slumbering upstairs. This didn't have anything to do with her. She was amazing and wonderful.

He was fucking confused.

What do I want to be when I grow up?

Or better yet…WHO do I want to be?

He didn't have the answers but he'd continue coming down early in the morning and thinking about it until he did.

"You're up early."

His wife's soft, sleepy voice pulled him from his melancholy thoughts. Turning from the rising sun outside, Maddie was rubbing at her eyes and yawning, her pajamas wrinkled and her hair askew.

She was the most beautiful, sexy woman he'd ever seen in his life, and he still had no earthly idea what she saw in him. Every day he was grateful to be the man by her side and he wanted to be sure she never regretted choosing him. She could have had someone far better, after all.

"I couldn't sleep," he answered, pulling her into his arms. She was warm and soft, her hair smelling like strawberries. "How about I pour you a cup of coffee?"

It wasn't her fault she'd interrupted his brooding. There was always tomorrow.

She yawned again but nodded, shuffling on bare feet to the

refrigerator. "I can make you breakfast if you want."

No. Just…no. He loved Madison with all his heart but she was without a doubt the worst cook in Montana. Maybe all of the states west of the Mississippi. She tried, bless her, but somehow everything ended up burnt, charred, mangled, or tasting like shoes. She was a brilliant doctor, but she needed to stay out of the kitchen.

"I'm on it, sweetheart. Besides, you'll be busy helping Amanda get ready. It's the big day, right?"

It was the first day of kindergarten for Amanda and both Maddie and his daughter had been talking about it all week.

His wife wrapped her hands around the warm coffee mug. "It is. Our daughter has spent the last two weeks picking out her first day outfit."

"She doesn't get that from me."

Giggling, Maddie shook her head. "She doesn't get that from me, either. I think she gets it from Aunt Sherry."

Amanda certainly adored her Aunt Sherry, Maddie's best friend. Sherry had twins the same age and his wife was thrilled to see a second generation growing up together.

"She gets her sunny disposition from me," Tanner declared with a grin. "She gets her brains and good looks from you."

Maddie sighed and reached for the box of cereal in the cabinet. "I certainly hope she doesn't go through the long, painful awkward phase that I went through. That was awful. Kids can be so cruel."

This wasn't the first time that his wife had mentioned not wanting anything bad to happen to Amanda when she started school. Maddie had been bullied and teased when she was a kid and he should know. He'd shooed several of them away one day and she'd thought of him as a hero after that.

Ten years of marriage should have solved that problem. He

was no hero and considering she'd scolded him the other day about leaving his socks on the floor – again – she had to know that now.

Her concern for Amanda was normal for a devoted mother but he didn't want her to have any unrealistic expectations. If he'd learned anything raising a son and a daughter who were now grown, it was that he couldn't protect them from everything. Even as much as he wanted to.

But he was smart enough not to lecture his wife about this topic. She didn't appreciate his *I've been around longer than you* speeches. In fact, she hated them. He'd didn't really like them either, as he didn't want to make a habit of reminding Maddie just how much older he was.

"Amanda will be fine," he assured her, dropping a kiss on her forehead before reaching into the drawer behind him for a spoon. The kitchen wasn't big enough for the two of them to maneuver comfortably. "She's a smart little girl and you're always telling her that she shouldn't care what other people think."

"That doesn't help when some mean boy is calling you carrot top," Maddie mumbled, accepting the spoon from Tanner and digging into her cereal. "Or pulling your hair. Or making fun of your freckles."

Quirking an eyebrow, he leaned down to press a kiss on Maddie's neck, the skin soft under his lips. "Freckles, huh? Clearly, that boy doesn't have good taste. I remember a night not too long ago when I showed you exactly what I think about your freckles."

His pretty wife's cheeks turned an adorable shade of red. She was remembering that night, too. He'd spent a great deal of time kissing every one of her freckles and was anxious to repeat that as soon as possible. Maybe even tonight.

Her hand pressed against his abdomen but she wasn't pushing him away, instead running it up his chest to rest on his shoulder. His sweet little innocent Maddie was actually a clever and wily seductress and he was her willing victim.

"You're so bad, Sheriff Marks," she whispered, a smile curving her full pink lips. "But I like the way your evil mind works."

"Irredeemably bad, that's me. I've got some more ideas if you're interested. What do you say, gorgeous?"

There was promise in her eyes and he was definitely going to take her up on it. "I'd like to hear about some of these ideas, Sheriff. How about meeting me at nine o'clock tonight? Upstairs?"

"It's a date."

Capturing her lips with his, he gave her a quick but thorough kiss. It was a down payment on later. Mornings weren't the best time for wooing. They always seemed to be in a rush.

"That's what I like to hear. I better go up and get a shower. I've got a big day ahead of me."

He placed his coffee cup on the counter and turned to go upstairs, but Maddie snagged the hem of his t-shirt, tugging him backward.

"I love you, Tanner."

He could see that love in her eyes when she looked at him just like she was at this moment. He was so damn grateful for the second chance he'd been given with this woman. That's why he felt guilty for...*contemplating* every morning. He shouldn't be restless or uncomfortable. He should just be grateful.

"I love you too, babe. More than you can ever know."

What the hell was wrong with him?

CHAPTER TWO

M addie had been looking forward to and dreading this morning all summer. She was excited that Amanda was starting school but there was a part of her – a huge part – that was mourning the loss of her *baby girl.*

It was silly, of course. Amanda was five, not twenty-five, and she was going to need her mother in many ways for years to come, but to Maddie this was a milestone that her daughter wasn't an infant or toddler any longer. She was a young girl and with that came all sorts of emotions she couldn't quite understand.

And Tanner didn't understand, either.

She hadn't mentioned it to him because she already knew what he was going to say.

Kids grow up. That's what they're supposed to do. He'd launched two children successfully into this big, bad world and he wasn't worried about doing it a third time. He was always so calm about everything, whether it was a scraped knee or a mean kid at the playground. It was all been there, done that.

Meanwhile, I'm a mess.

Not a big mess. More of a small one. Starting school wasn't

an insignificant day in Amanda's life, nor Maddie's, either. It didn't help that her forty-first birthday was just around the corner. Everything was moving so fast. She just wanted it to slow down – just for a minute – so she could catch her breath.

Was that too much to ask? Apparently so.

"I already packed my lunch, Mom."

Maddie paused, her hand in midair. She'd been about to retrieve Amanda's brand-new Disney princess lunchbox from the end of the counter, but her daughter's words had her mind going in fast forward.

"You did? When did you do that?"

I ask with fear in my heart. Please don't say last week and it was a tuna fish sandwich.

"Last night," Amanda answered. "While you and dad were running my bath."

Actually, they'd been kissing while running that bath and clearly not paying attention to their precocious five-year-old.

"Why don't you let me check to make sure you've got everything you need," Maddie suggested. "I don't want you to be hungry in the afternoon."

Amanda didn't like her lunch packing expertise to be called into question, her eyes sparkling with a bit of rebellion.

That she got from her father. In spades. Tanner didn't like being told what to do, either.

"It's fine, Mom."

"I'm sure it is. Will you just let me see what you packed? Is it a big secret?"

Maddie had visions of nothing but cookies and pudding packs. Amanda had a sweet tooth.

She got that from both of her parents.

With a sigh, Amanda opened her lunchbox for motherly inspection but didn't look too thrilled about it.

I didn't think I'd see that expression on her face until she was thirteen.

The contents weren't too bad. An apple and a banana. A juice box that was now warm from being out of the refrigerator all night. String cheese – also needing refrigeration. And a small bag of low-sodium pretzels. Basically, everything that Amanda liked to snack on.

"This looks okay. Don't you want a sandwich, though? And your drink and cheese need to be in the refrigerator until the morning. I have a cold pack that we can slip into your lunch."

It was shaped like a Dalmatian.

"Bread isn't good for you. I heard you say that to Aunt Sherry."

Maddie had worked hard not to have bad or good foods for her daughter. She didn't want to start any weird relationships with food, having seen some issues in her own patients. She'd simply said that some food should only be consumed in moderation.

What she'd said to Sherry wasn't far different. She remembered the conversation Amanda was referring to, but she didn't remember Amanda listening in. She'd have to be more aware from now on.

"What I said was that too much bread, or anything really, isn't good for you. A sandwich is fine if you want it. Two or three sandwiches is probably pushing it a little for someone your size."

Tall and skinny, just like Maddie had been.

"I don't want a sandwich. I want what I packed."

That little chin firmed and Maddie was well aware that her young daughter would put up a fight. Frankly, she didn't want today to be marred by a skirmish. The lunch wasn't that important in the big scheme of things. What had her own father said that first year after she'd given birth?

Pick your battles.

He'd been a terrific dad so he must know a thing or three.

"Fine, but let's get you a cold juice box and cheese."

To Maddie's relief, her daughter didn't argue and the rest of the morning went by smoothly and swiftly. Before she knew it, they were standing in front of Springwood Elementary. The very same school Maddie had attended all those years ago. It had been renovated at some point but for the most part it looked exactly as it had when she'd started kindergarten. Her mom had held her hand and she hadn't wanted to let it go, hanging back.

In contrast to Amanda who was tugging at Maddie's arm, urging her forward.

We're so different. She'll jump right in but I have to watch a bit first.

"There's Jack, Belle, and Aunt Sherry," Amanda said, giving her mother another big tug forward. "Let's go, Mom."

"Don't be in such a hurry," Maddie replied more sharply than she intended.

To grow up.

She took a deep breath and blew it out slowly. "What I mean is, there are a lot of cars in this parking lot. You need to be careful."

"I will be," Amanda promised, not paying a bit of attention to her mother. "Can we go now? There aren't any cars."

They crossed the long, curved driveway where parents were dropping off the older students. Since it was the first day, teachers were monitoring the area to make sure that all the children were headed in the right direction.

Sherry gave Maddie a huge grin when they approached, practically jumping up and down in excitement. "There you are. The twins can't wait to meet their new teacher."

Since there was only one kindergarten class in Springwood, Amanda, Jack, and Belle would all be in the same class. Just as

Maddie and Sherry had been thirty-six years ago.

Maddie appeared to be the only person in their little group who wasn't thrilled that it was the first day of school. Sherry and the kids kept up a lively chatter as they walked down the familiar corridors to the large open classroom. Their teacher had long ago retired but Mrs. Walker seemed like a lovely woman who truly loved children.

There were several rectangular tables in the middle of the room with centers set up along the periphery for reading, math, science, and social studies.

"Mom, there's a bunny!"

Before Maddie could stop her, Amanda had dropped her hand and was speeding toward a large cage in the corner. Luckily, Mrs. Walker must have seen it too, because before Amanda could open the cage the teacher was right by her side.

"Isn't he sweet?" Mrs. Walker asked with a smile. "His name is Benjamin. He belongs to the class."

Her mother completely forgotten, Amanda was entranced with the lop-eared rabbit. "Will we get to hold him?"

"Of course, but you have to learn how and be gentle. Everyone will get a chance to take him home for the weekend as well, but you have to have your parents' permission."

Amanda's eyes went wide and she turned to Maddie, a pleading tone in her voice. She'd been begging for a puppy all summer. If it had been up to Tanner, she would have had it months ago.

"Can I, Mom? Can I please?"

Now she remembers I'm here.

"I don't think this is the time to discuss it. We can do that later. I'm sure everyone is going to want a turn."

"I want a turn," Belle piped up, leaning her face against the cage. "Since Jack and I are twins do we get to have Benjamin two times?"

"Isabella," Sherry said sharply. "Is that a polite question?"

"No, Mom," Belle replied glumly. "I'm sorry, Mrs. Walker."

"Rabbits are dumb," Jack scoffed. "I'd rather have a lizard. They're cool."

"They aren't cool," Amanda said, her brows pinched together in a scowl. "They're not as cute as rabbits."

Whatever Mrs. Walker was being paid by the Springwood school district, it wasn't enough. She was definitely going to earn her money with these three in the class. Whenever they were together, they were a handful.

Mrs. Walker seemed to sense that a change in subject needed to happen right away.

"Can you find your names on your cubbies? Then you can put your things away and find your chair."

"I can read," Amanda said proudly, immediately finding hers. "And that's my chair. Belle and I are sitting together, Mom."

Sherry and Maddie exchanged a glance, remembering their own first day. They'd been sitting together, too. Maddie felt the emotion swelling inside, a lump forming in her throat and tears burning the backs of her eyes. She sniffled softly and knelt down to give her daughter a hug.

"That's great, isn't it? You and Belle will be together all day."

The bell rang and it was obviously time for the parents to leave. Mrs. Walker had taken a spot by the door to see everyone out and the students – with the help of a teacher's aide – had all found their seats.

There was nothing left to do but go.

Except that Maddie didn't want to.

I need more time. Just a few days more. Or a few weeks. I'm not ready.

But Amanda was, already giggling with Belle and enamored

with her classroom, teacher, and a bunny rabbit. Maddie couldn't even begin to compete with that.

Sherry linked her arm with Maddie's. "How about we get some coffee and a bear claw at the coffee shop? Do you have any early patients?"

"Not until ten."

"Then let's go celebrate the kids' first day of school. Coffee's on me."

Celebrate? Maddie wanted to sob.

Everything was moving far too fast.

CHAPTER THREE

"I'm getting too old for this shit," Tanner said as he and his deputy Sam entered the station house after answering a domestic abuse call. "I think people are getting crazier by the day."

Sam shook his head, pulling two cold sodas from the small refrigerator and tossing one to Tanner. "Naw, they were always like this but we were younger and more optimistic. Now we're older and cynical as hell."

Tanner couldn't argue with his friend. He *was* getting more cynical as he aged, but there didn't seem to be anything he could do to stop it.

Looking around the empty station house, Sam took a seat opposite Tanner. "Listen, I'm glad that we have a few minutes before the other guys get back here. There's something we need to talk about."

Tanner's gut tightened at Sam's words. He already knew what his best deputy was going to say.

"You need a raise," he said flatly. "I know you do and I've been talking to the mayor about it. All my men have gone too long without getting one. It's a travesty and it needs to be fixed as soon as possible."

Sam appeared relieved that Tanner understood. "It's been two years and I normally wouldn't say anything but Tabby and I are looking to add on to the house. The kids are getting bigger and we need more space."

Sam and Tabby had three boys under the age of eight and if anyone needed more room, it was them. Those kids had energy to spare and wore their parents half-ragged.

But there was something else going on today, not just a conversation about a raise that Sam should have been given long ago. The town budget was a mess but there was no excuse for not taking care of its first responders.

"You've had another offer," Tanner said, the thought popping into his head. "You're being recruited by another town."

From the look on Sam's face he'd hit the nail on the head. Dammit. Tanner didn't want to lose him. After all these years, he'd come to depend on Sam more than anyone else in the department but he was also aware that Sam could get a sheriff's job if he really wanted one.

"I don't want to take it," Sam replied, shaking his head again. "We don't want to move or uproot the kids. I want to make this situation work but…"

"But you need more money. I get it. And you deserve it."

"I know you haven't had a raise in over two years, either," Sam went on. "And all we read in the paper is about the tax base and how we don't have enough money to fix the roads or the schools or pay the cops or firefighters."

"The rich get richer and the poor get poorer," Tanner groused. "I don't see the fat cat businessmen tightening their belts. They're driving brand new cars and taking luxury vacations while most of the residents of this town work two or three jobs to make ends meet. Yet somehow the mayor always makes it sound like it's the little guy's fault that the roads are full of potholes and the kids don't have books in school."

Tanner didn't hold the current mayor in high regard. Or any regard at all, as a matter of fact. He didn't hate him because that would take energy that he didn't want to waste on the guy, but he thought the gasbag was a huge douche. The man sure could talk a lot but he never seemed to say much of anything. He was one of those people that had moved to Springwood in the last five years or so and thought the whole town was backward, needing *modernizing*. But their idea of modernizing was that a few guys make all the money and everyone else does all of the work.

"I know that you understand," Sam said. "I also know that what I'm asking is damn near impossible."

It shouldn't be. Getting a decent wage for his deputies shouldn't be like moving mountains.

"Let me talk to the mayor again. Let him know that we're losing deputies. Hell, maybe even I'll threaten to quit."

The mood he'd in lately, it didn't sound all that bad.

His declaration made Sam laugh. "Now that would make the mayor sweat. No one wants to see you go. You're an institution around here."

An institution? Some might be good, but others needed to be tore down.

Which one was he?

"It's going to be so amazing to have a few hours to myself during the day," Sherry marveled. "I'm even excited about cleaning the house."

Maddie and her best friend had found a quiet corner table in the local coffee shop. They were enjoying some French roast and a bear claw. Considering she'd had little sleep last night the caffeine was welcome and needed.

Eyes narrowed, Sherry tapped her chin. "Spill it. You've barely said two words all morning. What's going on?"

Not quite sure how to even begin describing her emotions, Maddie didn't reply right away. She hadn't spoken to Tanner or Sherry about this. They'd both seemed happy and excited about the first day of school.

But this was her best friend in the entire world and if anyone could understand it would be Sherry. And if she didn't understand she wouldn't make Maddie feel like a loser because of it.

"I think there's something wrong with me."

If her friend was surprised by her answer, she didn't let it show. She simply nodded and then took another sip of her coffee before speaking.

"I'm betting that there's something wrong with pretty much everyone. Can you be more specific?"

"I'm not happy about Amanda starting kindergarten." Realizing how that sounded, Maddie immediately backtracked. "Wait…that's not exactly what I meant. What I mean is that I'm happy, but I'm sad, too. It's just that she's growing up so fast and it feels like she was a baby only yesterday and now she's making her own lunch and picking out her own clothes and I'm going to blink my eyes and she'll be graduating high school and going off to college and I don't want her to leave, Sherry. It's just all moving so fast and I'm not ready for it."

The words had finally tumbled out, all of them jumbling together but Sherry didn't run away in horror.

"I don't want Belle and Jack to leave, either." Sherry smiled and patted Maddie's hand. "And yes, there's a part of me that's screaming that they're too little to start school and be away from me all day. They're just babies, right? What if one of them scrapes their knee and I'm not there to sing to them while I clean them up and put on the band-aid? Who's going to do that? But there's another part of me that's excited about all the stuff that they're going to do and see and experience. I'm still hoping Amanda goes to prom with Jack."

Sherry was always talking about that particular fantasy. And then they'd get married and they'd all be family.

"I'm not sure they're going to cooperate on that."

"What you're forgetting is that we get to experience it all again, too," Sherry said softly. "It's almost like getting a do-over but without the funny clothes and hairstyles."

That was an awful thought.

"I don't want to experience school again," Maddie said with a shudder. "It was horrible the first time. And what if the kids are mean to Amanda?"

Sherry's brows went up. "Then she'll probably kick them in the shin. Your little girl doesn't take any crap, if you haven't noticed."

"I noticed. She practically ran into the school this morning. She couldn't wait."

"Isn't that a good thing? That she's excited? Would you want her being scared and timid?"

"No, but…" Maddie buried her head in her hands. "I'm just not ready. It's all going so fast. I need it all to slow down."

Perhaps she'd be ready for Amanda to start school in a few months.

"It's not going to."

Such a simple but true statement. Sherry always did know how to sum up a situation.

"I know."

That was the crux of all of this. Nothing Maddie could do could change it. She could only hold on for the ride.

"I know what you mean, though," Sherry went on. "I told

Dan the other day that I was starting to get that baby-itch. He practically ran from the room covering his junk with his hands. It was hilarious. I know that we're not going to have any more kids. We're done. But I do miss that baby smell."

"That baby smell is heaven," Maddie agreed. "I miss it too. I miss rocking her to sleep. I miss teaching her the ABCs."

Sherry giggled, her eyes sparkling with mischief. "Don't worry. You'll be teaching all three of them fractions and algebra before too long. Lord knows, I can't help them with that. Luckily, I've never needed algebra in my day to day life. I did need geometry once when we bought flooring for the kitchen but it was only that one time."

Maddie didn't mention that Sherry and Dan still had several boxes of tile in their garage because they'd mis-measured and bought way too much.

"So you don't think I'm crazy?"

"You're crazy but in a really nice way. The kind of way that makes people love you. What does Tanner say about this? Is he feeling the same way?"

"I haven't said anything about this to him," Maddie admitted. "I don't think he'd understand. He seems so happy that she's starting school."

Although lately Tanner seemed...different. He'd been getting up before the sun and going downstairs, leaving her alone in their big bed. What was he doing? She didn't have a clue. He didn't know that she knew, either. But he'd been doing it every day since before the holidays. Eventually he'd talk about it, but until then she was trying to give him whatever space he needed.

"I'm sure he is but I bet he's feeling the passage of time, too. After all, he's a few years older than we are."

Maddie had never cared that Tanner was older than she was. For the most part, it hadn't made a bit of difference in their relationship, but it did sometimes have them on opposite sides of an issue. Her husband looked at life from a different perspective at times than she did.

"I'm just…I don't even know how to describe it. I'm *restless*, I guess, but I don't want things to change. I want everything to stay exactly the same and even as I say the words, I know how incredibly dumb and whiny I sound. Nothing stays the same and I'm normally fine with that. Why am I having such an issue now?"

Clearing her throat, Sherry shifted in her chair. "Do you think it has anything to do with a certain upcoming birthday? It's your forty-first."

As if I don't know.

"I'm not likely to forget that," Maddie replied, her tone testy. "Why would turning forty-one bother me? Forty didn't bother me and that was supposed to be this big milestone. It's just a number. And you're turning forty-one a week later, by the way. Maybe it's bugging you, not me. Have you thought of that?"

Sherry pointed to herself. "I'm not the one begging the universe to slow down. You are. It does bother me a little but I'm trying to ignore it. You're more cerebral than I am so it's not a surprise that you're thinking about it."

"I'm not thinking about it."

"I think that you are. I think that you're going through an early mid-life crisis."

"A mid-life crisis," Maddie repeated. "That's absurd."

Right?

"It's just a suggestion. You're the doctor here. What would you tell someone who came into your office complaining that she was tired–?"

"I didn't say I was tired."

"But you are, aren't you? You're always yawning."

"Yes, but I work a lot."

"Okay, she says she's tired all the time and she wants the world to slow down and she's restless, but she doesn't want anything to change. What would you say?"

What would I say? Physician, heal thyself.

Maddie sighed. "I'd tell her to eat right, get plenty of rest, exercise if she wasn't already, and to try a change of scenery. Shake up her routine a little."

"So now you know what you have to do."

No. No, no, no. Whenever Sherry had that look on her face it was trouble. The last time Maddie had seen that expression her friend had been finding her a husband. Tanner.

That hadn't turned out so badly but this had trouble written all over it.

"I don't like change."

"You need to embrace it. You're stuck in a mid-life rut. When was the last time you did anything that you hadn't planned ahead of time?"

"I'm not ready."

"No time like the present."

"I hate you."

"You love me. Now…where do we start? I know…yoga. It's great for centering the mind. You can come to class with me tomorrow."

"I have work."

"I go in the evening after the kids are in bed. You'll sleep like a baby afterward. I promise."

"I don't want to."

"This is why you're in a rut. I'm going to help you out of it."

"Actually, I'm feeling much better," Maddie said, forcing a huge smile to her face. "I'm happy and content with life. No problems here. Just talking to you made all the difference."

"I'm not taking no for an answer. We're going to shake you out of your mid-life crisis."

Maddie had been here before. Resistance was futile.

Her only option was to close her eyes, jump, and hope that the fall wouldn't kill her.

Tanner didn't waste any time after his talk with Sam. He called the mayor's office and told Geri, the secretary that he wanted to talk to him right away. No excuses. He was surprised when Geri informed him that the mayor was on his way to the station house already. She didn't know why but he should be there any minute.

With not much time to prepare what he needed to say, Tanner scribbled down a few points that he wanted to make sure to cover when they met. The first one being that they were dangerously close to losing Sam.

It wasn't long after that Mayor Pete Carlisle walked in and headed straight for Tanner's office, barely glancing at anyone, and shutting the door behind him. He looked pale and pinched but that was par for the course with Pete. The man was never happy and constantly looked like he was constipated. If that's what being rich did to a man, Tanner would happily stay middle class.

"Pete, I just called and talked to Geri. We need to talk."

Nodding, the mayor sat down on the chair opposite Tanner and then jumped up and began to pace the small space between the desk and the door.

"She sent me a text about that. I don't really have time—"

"We have to talk," Tanner broke in. "I won't let you put me off this time. If we're not careful we're going to lose Sam, my best deputy. You need to look into that budget of yours and find some money for raises for these hardworking men and women who put their lives on the line every day. I've lost four deputies this year due to salary issues and we can't lose any more."

It wasn't the carefully planned speech that he had in mind but Pete was being especially difficult today.

The mayor stopped and fidgeted with his tie. "It might be for the best, Tanner. If your deputy has another offer–"

"We can't let him go. He's second in command around here and has years of experience."

Gripping the back of the chair, Pete sighed. "I wanted to do this differently, Tanner. I was hoping we could come to some arrangement and perhaps announce your retirement."

My retirement? What the hell?

Tanner didn't like what he was hearing, and Pete looked like he was about to pass out.

"Why would I retire?"

The man pulled a handkerchief out of his pocket and dabbed at his forehead. "Because things are changing and you're not."

This was a bunch of bullshit.

"What you're saying is that you want to change things and I'm not going to like it."

The back of his neck was hot with anger. This little weasel was trying to pull something.

"Costs are out of control–"

"Bull crap."

"And I feel we could do better with a privatization plan–"

"Fuck that."

Pete heaved a sigh and looked down at the floor before speaking again.

"Tanner, I'm taking this town in a new direction. A better direction. We're going to make the budget lean so that we can be nimble–"

"More bullshit-speak." Tanner leaned across the desk, his hands flat on the dark, scarred oak. His three predecessors had used this same desk. It had history, something this guy wouldn't understand. "Spit it out, Pete."

"Fine," the mayor said loudly, his lips flattened into a line. "You're fired, Tanner. Fired. I'm bringing in someone younger. You have until the end of the day to clean out your desk."

Fired? What the fuck did that even mean?

CHAPTER FOUR

A busy day seeing patients took Maddie's mind off all of her issues but it all came rushing back when it was time to pick up Amanda from school. Going forward, Sherry would pick up all three of the kids but on this important first day Maddie wanted to do it herself. She wanted to hear all of the exciting activities her daughter had done today, plus she and Sherry had decided to take their new kindergarteners for ice cream as a first day of school treat.

Because I'm happy that she started school.

And I'm comfortable with how quickly she's growing up.

At some point during the day, Maddie had decided that the power of positive thinking just might do the trick. Instead of allowing herself to wallow in a quagmire of questions and few answers, she needed to buck up and be optimistic. Look forward to all the great changes that were coming her way. Sherry was thrilled that her twins were starting school and Maddie was determined to do the same.

They met at the ice cream parlor and it was hot fudge sundaes all around. The kids were chattering excitedly about their day – Benjamin the rabbit, the story Mrs. Walker had read, the art project, and of course recess.

"Recess was my favorite," Sherry laughed, wiping a bit of whipped cream from Jack's cheek. "I liked art, too. Maddie liked math."

Sighing, Maddie nodded in agreement. "I did, I admit it. I thought it was cool. No one else did, though."

The bell over the ice cream parlor door rang and Clarice Daugherty walked in with her three kids. Sherry and Maddie waved and the other woman promptly strode over to their table.

"Oh my gosh, Maddie. I didn't expect to see you here," she said in a hushed tone, glancing around the store. "You're so brave and strong. I'd be a mess."

What? Did everyone know about how she was dealing with Amanda's first day of school? Sherry would never in a million years tell anyone.

Giving her best friend a look, Sherry's eyes widened and she shrugged. She didn't know what Clarice was talking about, either.

"It's only the first day of school," Maddie finally replied. "I'm sure I'll be fine."

Clarice's forehead wrinkled, her brows pulled down. "I'm not talking about that. I'm talking about Tanner getting fired today. You're taking it really well. How's he doing? I can't even imagine this town without him as the sheriff."

Maddie had never seen Sherry's eyes that large and round. She could only imagine her expression right now because inside she was a mess. Her stomach roiled, almost immediately wanting to purge the chocolate mint ice cream with hot fudge sauce, and a sweat broke out on the back of her neck. She actually felt faint.

But there was no way she was going to let Clarice know.

"We're fine," she said, although she was in no way okay. "Everything is fine."

"What's fired mean?" Jack piped up, shoving another spoonful of ice cream into his mouth. Sherry shushed him, and distracted the kids by pointing out a dog walking down the sidewalk.

Clarice said something else that Maddie didn't hear, the blood roaring in her ears and blocking out sound, before being pulled away by her kids wanting their ice cream.

When she was finally out of earshot, Maddie pressed a hand to her forehead. It was damp with sweat. Then she checked her phone to make sure she hadn't missed any calls or texts from her husband.

No. None. What the hell?

"Maybe Clarice has a drinking problem," Sherry suggested. "She's always been a little flighty."

"Clarice doesn't have a drinking problem. Her husband works at the town hall. He must have told her."

Sherry shook her head. "Tanner would call you if something like this happened. There's no way Clarice has this right. She's confused. Worst case scenario, Tanner got mad and quit. The mayor would never fire him."

Maddie didn't know what Pete Carlisle would do. She did think Tanner would have told her but he'd been acting strangely lately. Not like himself.

"Perhaps he did quit," Maddie said softly so the children wouldn't hear. Luckily, they were busy giggling and eating and not too interested in the drama among the adults. "He's been acting different these last few months."

"You didn't tell me that."

"I know," Maddie admitted. "It's not anything that I can put my finger on. He's just acting a little differently, that's all."

"If you want to run home and talk to him, I can take Amanda with me for a few hours. It's no trouble."

That was an offer Maddie was enthusiastically going to accept.

Tanner Marks, just what is going on?

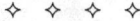

Tanner was in the kitchen chopping garlic when he heard Maddie at the front door. His stomach twisted in his gut at the sound of her footsteps on the hardwood floor. Fast and unhappy. He was probably going to be sleeping on the couch tonight, and it was his own fault. He should have called her after his meeting with the mayor but just how did a man tell his wife that he got fired?

He'd been thinking about that all afternoon and he still didn't have an answer.

Which was why he was about to get his ass handed to him by his wife.

Maddie breezed into the kitchen and dumped her handbag on the table. The color was high on her cheeks and her eyes sparkled with anger. Whew, she was mad. He didn't even get a chance to step forward and greet her before she was firing a question at him.

"Tanner, is there something you want to tell me?"

Want? No. Need? Yes. Time to talk, whether he wanted to or not. He didn't like this feeling in the least. The smell of the spaghetti sauce he was cooking was making him queasy.

"Yes, I do need to talk to you."

Her brows raised, she waited for him to say more. That was one of Maddie's best qualities. She was a good listener.

Now she was going to hear what a loser her husband was.

"I had a meeting with the mayor today. I wanted to discuss raises for the deputies. He had another agenda altogether. He said he wanted to bring in someone younger. I was let go from my job."

There. He'd said it.

Maddie blew out a long breath, her shoulders slumped. "Why didn't you call me?"

This time he did step in closer, wrapping his arms around her and pulling her against his body. For the first time today, he was at peace. She, on the other hand, was stiff as a board.

"I wanted to but every time I picked up the phone to do it, I didn't know what to say."

"I had to hear it from Clarice at the ice cream shop. Can you imagine how I felt, Tanner? Let me tell you. I felt like an idiot. Sherry was there and so were the kids."

Shit, it was worse than he'd imagined.

"Where's Amanda?"

"With Sherry. I'll pick her up in a few hours." Maddie looked up, tears pooled in her eyes. "Are you okay? What happened exactly?"

She wanted a play by play of his meeting? Fuck.

"It was just like I told you. I went there to discuss salaries for the deputies and Pete told me that he wanted to make some changes. I needed to clean out my desk by the end of the day."

Surprisingly, after all of these years Tanner hadn't had all that much personal crap at the station. It had only taken a few minutes and one copy paper box.

Her brows were knitted together. "How did you get home? I didn't see your truck out front."

That. He hadn't explained *that* yet.

"Maybe I should start at the beginning."

"Maybe you should."

She didn't sound happy. He was definitely sleeping on the couch tonight. He'd fucked up royally. He and Maddie didn't argue much, both of them pretty laid back, but she was understandably pissed off. If only he knew the magic words to make it all better. Sadly, he didn't. They were going to have to fight this one out.

"It all started with my conversation with Sam."

❖   ❖   ❖   ❖

They'd ended up sitting at the kitchen table while Tanner explained his day in excruciating detail. Maddie had a bunch of questions, of course, and he'd tried to answer them without sounding like a huge loser.

"You have a severance package?"

Tanner wasn't sure he'd called it a package. More like a paper bag.

"A week of pay for every year that I've been with the town of Springwood. Capped at eight weeks. It's the standard in the contract."

He'd always known it but he'd never thought he'd have to deal with it. He'd been short-sighted, obviously.

Maddie leaned her chin on her hand. "It's not a big deal. Financially we're fine."

Because of Maddie's money, and the fact that her father had gifted them this house. They hadn't had a mortgage payment so they'd been able to save more than most people.

Which was good because...

"The SUV belongs to the city. I had to turn it in today."

Her eyes widened but then she nodded in understanding. "Right. Of course. You've been driving it so long I'd forgotten. I guess we need to get you a vehicle right away."

"I already called Hal down at the dealership. They have a used truck with low miles. I told him I'd be by in the morning."

Maddie's eyes narrowed. "You called Hal?"

"I did."

Apparently, that had been a bad move on his part. Maddie's

cheeks were red again.

"What else did you do after you were fired?"

"I talked to Sam and Tabby for a little while. The guys quit in protest, which I told them they shouldn't do. Hell, they need those jobs. But they said it was the principle of the thing."

Principles didn't pay the grocery bill, though.

"Tabby? You talked to her?"

"Yes."

It was beginning to dawn on Tanner why his lovely wife was getting even angrier.

"Anyone else?"

He shook his head. "I stopped at the grocery store to pick up supplies for spaghetti tonight."

Maddie placed her hands on the table, the fingers splayed out, studying her nails. "Let me get this straight. You were fired and then you talked to Hal, Sam, and Tabby. You went to the grocery store, probably talking to a few people there, too. Then you came home and started dinner, and at no time did you manage to call or text me? Do I have this right or have I missed anything? Because I don't want to miss anything."

"I know I've fucked up, babe. Really badly," Tanner replied in a rush, wanting to get back in the good graces of the woman he loved. "I just couldn't tell you that I'd been fired."

"But you could tell all those other people?"

He took a deep breath before answering. "Because their opinions of me don't mean squat compared to yours. I'm so very sorry, Maddie. I wanted to tell you but I just didn't know how to admit that I'd lost my job. Please forgive me."

In his first marriage Tanner had learned how to argue. In his second, older and wiser, he'd learned that most things weren't worth fighting about. It didn't hurt to apologize as much as it had when he was younger. Especially when he knew that he was in the wrong.

"Please don't do it again," she finally said with a sigh. "I understand what you're saying but hearing it from Clarice—"

"Sucked," he broke in. "It was wrong and I have no good defense. Just an explanation. I've never been fired before and I didn't know what I was supposed to do."

"You're supposed to tell your wife. First. Right away. Before all the gossips in this small town do it for you. We don't live in Chicago."

"I don't think I was really thinking, to be honest. I was reacting."

"I don't think less of you for being fired, Tanner. It happens to a lot of people."

"Have you ever been fired?"

For the first time this afternoon, Maddie appeared to relax, a smile curving her lips.

"Yes, and I deserved it, too. I was waitressing while in college and I was terrible at it. Just awful. I kept breaking dishes and mixing up orders. I lasted three long days before they put me out of my misery. It's not like your situation. You're great at your job. You were fired over politics. That Pete Carlisle wants to change Springwood into something neither of us would recognize."

That was true.

"So am I forgiven? Or at least partially forgiven?"

"Don't do it again."

He sure as hell wasn't planning on getting fired for a second time.

"I won't."

"So what are you going to do now?"

Good question. Excellent question.

He didn't have an answer, though.

"I'm not sure. Get a new vehicle." His gaze wandered over the kitchen. "There's a few projects that need doing around the house. This might be my chance to finally get them done before I start looking for another job."

That I'm not qualified for. I've never done anything but be a cop.

He wasn't prepared for a job search at this point in his life. After the military he'd become a deputy and then the sheriff. This was it. This was all he knew how to do.

"It might be a good idea to take some time off and figure out what you want to do," Maddie said. "You've hardly had any time off and we're fine financially. Take the opportunity to do whatever you want."

The problem was he had no idea what he wanted to do. He only knew that this change wasn't what he'd wanted but it was here. Now he had to deal with it.

What do I want to be when I grow up? The revised edition.

CHAPTER FIVE

H and on doorknob, Maddie took a deep breath before entering the house. It had been ten days since Tanner had been fired and he had certainly made the most of his time off.

By ripping apart the house.

She simply hadn't known that when he'd spoken about a few home improvement projects that needed to be done that he'd go quite this far. The kitchen was in a shambles, the dryer was in several pieces, and Tanner would walk around the house wearing a tool belt and muttering about the next project he wanted to tackle.

And she'd be fine with that if only he'd finish the ones that he'd already started.

She hadn't said anything to him, of course. It didn't seem nice or polite. After all, he thought he was *helping*. Plus, he'd already been through so much with losing his job that she hated to say anything negative to him if she could help it.

In many ways it was wonderful to have him home more. He dropped Amanda off and picked her up at school, allowing Maddie to start seeing patients earlier in the day, which meant getting home earlier, too. He always had dinner cooking when she came home and since she could barely boil water that was great. When Tanner had been working, she and Amanda had eaten out quite a bit. Even her young daughter knew that Mom's cooking sucked.

She pushed open the door and braced herself for whatever she found on the other side, giving herself a pep talk as she did it. It's not that bad. It was only temporary. Just until Tanner went back to work. He'd worked hard his entire life and he deserved some time off to rest and relax.

There was only one problem with that statement. Tanner seemed determined to do everything but rest and relax. He was up before the sun and busy around the house almost every minute of the day.

"Tanner," she called as she stepped in the door. "I'm home."

The mouthwatering smell of pot roast hit her nostrils and her stomach growled. It had been far too many hours since she'd fed it. She'd grabbed a sandwich and some pretzels in between patients.

The sound of tiny feet across the floor and then Amanda ran into Maddie's legs, her short arms wrapped around her mother's waist.

"Mommy, you're home."

Before Maddie could agree that she was, indeed, home, her daughter launched into a long soliloquy about her day. They'd played games, and read books, and worked on their addition skills. Like her mom, Amanda loved math.

"And we went to the library," the new kindergartener said. "They let me check out two books."

"That's great. We can read them tonight before bed."

"I've already read them. With Daddy."

"We read them after snack."

Tanner's deep voice still sent shivers up Maddie's spine all these years later. Somehow her husband managed to get more handsome with age. She often teased him about making a deal with the devil. He'd just laugh and say that the devil was terrified of him.

He was wearing that tool belt again, though.

A glance towards the sink told the tale. He'd pulled apart the faucet a few days ago and it was still in pieces.

He seemed to pick up on her thoughts, his own gaze following hers. "The faucet is on backorder. Should be in on Monday."

The last three nights they'd washed the dishes in the laundry room.

"That's good. How was your day?"

"Busy. I worked on the baseboards in the living room."

"The baseboards," Maddie echoed, her heart sinking. "I didn't know we had a problem with them."

"They were old and original to the house, I'm guessing."

Maddie had never noticed the baseboards in any room of the house. Did baseboards get old? How did one tell that they were aging and needed replacing?

"Probably they were," she replied. "I didn't even realize they needed replaced."

"The new ones I'm putting in will look better. They're higher and slightly more ornate." He unhooked the belt and laid it on the kitchen table. "But then I thought that this would be a really good time to paint the living room too, before I install the new baseboards."

It sounded like a reasonable plan. Except that he had several projects already in the works.

"You're going to paint the living room?"

I ask with real fear in my heart.

"Might as well while I have the baseboards pulled off. I think it will really spruce up the room. I have some paint colors for you to look at. Once you choose, I can pick up the paint the next day."

He'd reached into a drawer behind him and now he was holding a stack of little cards out to her, his expression expectant. These were the paint colors, apparently.

Now? I just walked in the door.

"How about I look at them after dinner?"

"Great." He set the cards on the counter. "I have to make a trip to the hardware store tomorrow anyway so it all works out."

From what Maddie could tell, Tanner had made a trip to the hardware store every single day since he'd been fired. Okay, maybe not that first day but every day after that.

"Can I see, Daddy? I want to help pick out the colors."

Amanda's plaintive tone pulled Maddie from her reverie. Her daughter was a girly-girl and loved to look at colors, and pillows, and fabric. She was going to be disappointed, however, as Maddie was planning on painting their beige living room…beige. If she was feeling wild? Perhaps a taupe. The furniture, pillows, and rugs had lots of color and anything else on the walls would be far too busy.

"Of course, you can look," Maddie assured her daughter. "But we're not going to paint the living room pink. That's a special color just for your room."

It looked like a princess and a unicorn had exploded in there. Pink, purple, and glitter. Every little girl's dream. Maddie's own childhood bedroom had been very much like it.

"How about you soak in a nice hot tub after your day at work?" Tanner suggested. "I'll clean up what I was working on and finish up dinner."

"I can help—"

"I got it. Go relax. You've had a long day."

He never accepted her offers for help in the kitchen. She

didn't blame him; she really sucked at cooking and he was so good at it. Still, it didn't seem fair.

"Then I'll do the dishes after," she said, setting her purse on the little table by the door along with her keys. "Give me twenty minutes."

"Take all the time you need. I've got plenty to do here. Amanda's going to help me."

Tanner was going to need more than a five-year-old to clean all of this up. He was going to need a magic wand.

And magic and miracles were in short supply these days.

"When were you going to call me?"

Logan Wright's blunt question was the first thing Tanner heard when he answered his phone. No hello. No greeting. No polite pleasantries. But that was Logan. Tanner considered it one of his friend's better qualities as the man could always be counted on to tell it like it was.

"Nice to hear from you too, Logan," Tanner laughed. He poured Amanda a cup of juice and set it on the table where she was working on a coloring book while he finished fixing dinner. "It's been awhile."

It had been about six weeks. They tried to keep in touch as much as possible but it wasn't easy with their crazy schedules and family commitments.

"Why didn't you call me?"

It wasn't a complex question but Tanner wasn't sure how to answer one of his best friends in the entire world. It wasn't that he was ashamed and didn't want Logan to know. If anyone understood small town politics it would be Logan Wright. It was...

Dammit, it was that restlessness again. That feeling of not

being quite comfortable and not sure what he was doing or even why he was doing it. Tanner had always been a decisive man, so this whole phase he was going through was really beginning to piss him off. If this was a mid-life crisis, it sucked. Could he just buy a red convertible and be done with it?

"I guess you heard the good news then."

"I should have heard it from you." Logan sounded peeved. Too bad. "Why didn't you call me? We can have your paperwork done and have you back on the job in less than a week."

That's exactly what Tanner was afraid of. For some reason that he couldn't quite fathom, he wasn't sure he wanted to be a lawman anymore. Even in the consulting capacity for Logan's firm.

He wasn't sure of anything and that was the problem.

"I'm not in a hurry to go back to work," Tanner finally replied, keeping his tone neutral. "I have a million projects around the house and frankly, I wanted some damn downtime. I'm not getting any younger and I didn't want to turn around and go straight back to work."

Not that Tanner had been letting himself rest. Since he didn't know what he wanted to do, he'd been riding himself to keep busy so he wouldn't sit and brood about all the questions swirling in his head.

"Shit, you can take all the time you want," Logan said. "We. can set your start date any time in the future. We're just so fucking glad that you're available now."

Logan, Jared, and Jason had been busting Tanner's balls for the last few years, trying to get him to resign as sheriff of Springwood and come work for them. They'd basically promised him anything he wanted and he could name his price. He'd been sorely tempted but his responsibility to the town had kept him from accepting. Then there was Maddie and Amanda. He didn't want to travel and be away from home too often. He'd already blown Emily and Chris's childhoods, and he didn't want to do it again. He'd vowed that this time he'd be present and sober.

And speaking of Chris… He wasn't too sure that his son would welcome having his old man working at the same place.

His sweet Maddie had always said that she'd support whatever decision he made. She wanted him to be happy and that life was too short to work at a job he didn't like. But he still hadn't pulled the trigger and made the switch. Something had kept him where he was.

So he could get fired by that rat faced mayor.

Realizing that he hadn't responded to Logan, Tanner tried to be diplomatic. *Don't burn any bridges, but don't make any commitments, either.*

"I just want to enjoy myself for now and figure out the future when it's time. I don't want to rush into anything."

There was a small silence before Logan spoke again.

"That's wise, actually." Another pause. "Are you thinking of retiring?"

Was he? It wasn't out of the question. He was fifty-five years old and he hadn't planned to do anything of the sort a few weeks ago. He'd assumed that he'd work another ten years but clearly the universe was telling him to make other plans.

"It's something I'm thinking about. I'm not getting any damn younger."

Logan laughed. "None of us are. But I have to be honest with you, I can't imagine you retired. You're just not the type. Shit, you don't even play golf. You'd go crazy within a few months."

"Not having enough to do would be an interesting problem to have. Right now, I'm keeping busy with some projects around the house."

Every time Tanner looked around his home, he saw something that needed to be done. He'd been negligent in maintaining their house for too long and he intended making up for that.

"I wouldn't mind spending some time with my wife," he added. "It seems we never have enough time together."

"That's what you should do. Take Maddie on a tropical vacation," Logan urged. "Somewhere, just the two of you. Get some sun, sit on the beach, maybe go parasailing or some shit like that. Just relax. I bet by the time you get back you'll know if you want to retire or not. Even if you don't, you'll be rested and refreshed. You should do it. Isn't Maddie's birthday coming up? That would be a hell of a surprise present."

Maddie was turning forty-one, not that she seemed to be bothered by that. She looked ten years younger, so why would she be?

They'd also never really treated themselves to a big vacation since their honeymoon. Jobs and then family always seemed to take priority. Perhaps Logan was right and he'd be in a much better frame of mind when he came back as well. Then he could make all the decisions that needed to be made.

"For a man as dumb as a rock, that's not a bad suggestion," Tanner joked. "A week away, just the two of us, may be just what the doctor ordered. I can talk to her friend Sherry and see what she suggests."

Sherry knew Maddie almost as well as she knew herself. If she thought Maddie wanted a surprise trip for her birthday, she'd say so. If she thought it was a lousy idea, she'd say that, too.

"Every now and then I get a little wood on the ball," Logan said with a chuckle. "Women love romantic shit. And there's nothing more romantic than sweeping her off of her feet and taking her on a trip she didn't have to plan, right?"

This just might be the answer to two problems. Maddie's birthday and Tanner's restlessness.

One romantic, carefree getaway coming right up.

CHAPTER SIX

"Do I get a lollipop if I don't make a fuss?" Sherry asked with a nervous laugh as she settled onto the patient's table in Maddie's office. She was here for a flu shot. "I think I should get a cocktail instead."

Sherry hated needles. Flu shot needles. Knitting needles. She didn't care which, she just hated them. Every year she and Maddie did this dance where Sherry would come in for her shot and Maddie would have to calm her down. What should take about two minutes usually took a good half hour of Sherry moaning and groaning and generally being a fraidy-cat. She always came alone because she didn't want anyone to witness her fright.

"It's nine-thirty in the morning," Maddie reminded her friend, pulling on a pair of gloves. "A little early for hard liquor but I don't judge. Do you want to do some of those imaging exercises we tried last year?"

It hadn't really helped, but then the only thing that really had was the year Sherry was already taking pain pills for a broken ankle. Then she hadn't cared about the needle, and she probably wouldn't have cared if Maddie had sawed off her leg, to be honest.

"No, I want you to just do it fast and get it over with. Don't draw this out. Just do it."

"This is a new approach," Maddie observed. "What brought this wave of bravery on?"

"Watching my kids get their shots," Sherry replied. "I tell them that the quicker it happens, the quicker they can get over it. I do it with band-aids, too."

"It is the best way. Get it done and move on. Is that really what you want me to do?"

Sherry nodded, her teeth sinking down into her bottom lip. She squeezed her eyes shut as Maddie swabbed down the area with alcohol and as quickly and gently as possible administered the shot. It was over in seconds.

"Shit, that hurt." Sherry's eyes filled with tears and her lips trembled. "God, I hate getting shots. It's archaic. Why can't medical science find a better way? There has to be a more humane way to give the flu vaccine."

"Modern medicine is working on it. You did great, though. I think this new approach is the way to go. Very efficient. I expected this to take much longer."

"Then do you have time for a cup of coffee?"

Maddie checked the clock on the wall. "My next patient shows up in twenty minutes."

They slipped into the kitchen where there was a full pot of coffee, cheerfully made by Maddie's amazing office admin Cheryl.

"So how is Tanner doing? Still on the home improvement bandwagon?"

Rolling her eyes, Maddie groaned. "He's pulled the base-boards off of the living room walls and now he wants to repaint as well. And the faucet in the kitchen is still in pieces, too. If he doesn't go back to work soon, I'm not sure what will be left of the house. He can't sit for more than ten minutes at a time."

"Did you say anything to him about it?"

"Absolutely not. He's acting like getting fired doesn't bother him but I think that it really does. I think he wanted to go out on his own terms. I've encouraged him to rest and relax but he doesn't seem to know how after all these years."

"So what are you going to do?"

That was an excellent question. If only Maddie had the answer.

"I don't know," she confessed. "I want him to be happy but I don't think that he is right now. I've never told you but even before he lost his job, he would wake up really early and come downstairs. He thought I was asleep but I knew. He's been doing it for months and I don't know why. Something has to be bothering him but I have no clue what it is. He didn't have any complaints about work – at least no new ones, his kids are fine, he's fine, I'm fine, and Amanda is great. So why is he getting out of bed early every morning?"

Sherry shrugged. "Maybe he just wants a few minutes of peace and quiet before his day starts. It doesn't seem like a big deal to me."

It wouldn't. But there was a time when waking up early meant that Tanner and Maddie could have a morning lovemaking session. Special time for the two of them. Now it seemed he wanted his time alone. Without her. It hurt. More than she wanted to admit.

"And you're feeling restless and like things are moving too fast," Sherry went on. "Maybe he is, too. He's older than us, remember? I would imagine he'd love to slow down time a little bit. Maybe in those early mornings it all feels better."

That…made sense. She'd assumed that Tanner wouldn't be

bothered by all of that – he was always so calm and mature – but perhaps she'd assumed wrong.

"I'm just going to give him the space he needs," Maddie replied. "And encourage him to relax a little bit."

Sherry's eyes went wide and she was practically bouncing up and down. "You two should go on a second honeymoon. It would be so romantic and then he'll have to relax, right? I can watch Amanda while you're gone. It would be no trouble at all. In fact, the twins are better behaved when she's there than when she's not, so you'd be doing me a favor."

A trip with only the two of them. It would be lovely, and something they hadn't done in years. But…

"I can't just dump my child on you and leave."

"You're not dumping her. You're leaving her with Aunt Sherry who adores her. And let's face it, she adores me. We'll have fun. It will be fine. It's one week out of her life. You're not abandoning her."

Still…

"I'm not even sure Tanner will go."

"Make him go. Tell him that you need the time off, too. Make it happen. You need a can-do attitude here."

"It would be nice," Maddie sighed. "I'd love to get away. But where?"

"Does it matter? You'll be together. But if it were me, I'd go somewhere tropical and warm. No wait…maybe back to Las Vegas. We had such a good time there."

Sherry and Dan had been married in Vegas. Maddie and Tanner had attended and it had been their first trip together.

But Sherry still wasn't finished. "No wait…New York City. You could take in the sights and see a Broadway show. No, hold on, you should go to Europe. Maybe London or Paris or Rome. I'd go to Paris with Dan in a heartbeat."

The world was their oyster, so to speak. A romantic vacation for two sounded like exactly what they needed.

Could she convince Tanner to go?

Tanner was only trying to get a hot cup of coffee after a trip to the hardware store but it simply wasn't to be. He'd gathered a crowd in the diner and couldn't get to the door to get the hell out of there.

"I told Pete Carlisle that he's lost my vote in the next election," Ted Simpson griped, slamming his hand on the counter. "What was he even thinking?"

Archie Walls nodded his head up and down in agreement. As a matter of fact, all the heads in the group were nodding and there was about a dozen people there complaining. He'd heard it all before, though. The residents of Springwood were not happy about the changes. Tanner was trying to be as neutral as possible, not wanting to seem bitter about being let go.

He didn't want that little peckerhead Pete Carlisle to think that he'd upset him in any way. What an asshole.

"That's what I told him, too. He's made a big mistake and is going to pay the price come voting day. I had a break-in at the store two days ago and it took his low-budget deputy eight hours to get there. When I asked where the hell he'd been, he said he was the only one on duty. Can you believe that? What in the hell is Pete spending my tax dollars on, anyway? It ain't on the cops, that's for sure."

"Mark my word," Ted Simpson said with another slap to the counter to punctuate his statement. "When one of the buildings or houses in town burns down or somebody gets hurt, he's not going to be able to explain what the hell he was thinking. The man's an idiot, and a dangerous one."

After seeing the effects of what Pete had implemented, Tanner wouldn't be arguing with Ted and Archie. The mayor had cut the police and fire departments to the bone and no one in Springwood was better off or safer for it. It was a foolhardy and stupid thing to do and something bad was bound to happen eventually.

And just what was Pete spending all their tax dollars on? That was a question that had been rattling around in Tanner's head for the last week.

"We're going to get an election recall," Archie declared. "And kick him out of office."

Taking a gulp of his coffee, Tanner rubbed at his chin. He'd always tried to be the voice of reason in any room but even his patience was running short these days.

"Have you talked to Pete about it yet?" he asked. "Told him your concerns?"

Ted and Archie exchanged a glance and the others that had been silent were now all staring that the floor.

Shit. He knew how this turned out.

"We were hoping you would talk to him," Ted finally said. "Make him see reason."

That was about the last thing Tanner wanted to do.

He cleared his throat. "About that, I'm not sure he's going to listen to me much. He did fire me, after all, so I don't think he's looking for my opinion about anything. Can't you call a town meeting? If you have enough signatures, he has to hold one. It's in the town charter."

From the expression on the men's faces, they'd all forgotten that little tidbit. It hadn't been used in over a decade as far as Tanner could remember, but it was there for situations just like this one.

A grin spread across Archie's face. "This is why we need you to be sheriff, Tanner. I'd forgotten about the town charter. It has provisions in it to recall the mayor, if I remember correctly and the ability to do it in a speedy fashion. That's what we need. Get a new mayor and get you and your men back to work."

Tanner should have been joyous at those words but he didn't feel the expected rush of happiness. This mid-life crisis crap really sucked. What was happening to him?

The bell over the door rang and Sherry walked in. Perfect timing. He needed to talk to her and he also needed to remove himself from this clearly pissed off group of town residents. Everyone was coming to him with their complaints and there wasn't a damn thing he could do to fix it all.

"Excuse me, I need to speak to Sherry."

Tanner sidestepped Ted and Archie and was able to intercept Sherry as she accepted a to-go cup of coffee and a Danish.

"Do you have a minute?" Tanner requested. "I promise it won't take long."

"You can take as long as you like," she replied with a smile. "The kids are in school and I'm heading off to grocery shop. Never shop on an empty stomach."

She held up the Danish.

Giving the angry crowd a sideways glance, he motioned for Sherry to follow him to a quieter corner.

"I was thinking of taking Maddie on a little vacation. Just the two of us. So I was hoping you could watch Amanda and I was also hoping that you could give me some ideas as to where she might like to go."

Sherry's eyes lit up and she awkwardly tried to clap her hands together without dropping her coffee and Danish. "That's the best idea of heard of in…well…since this morning. It's a wonderful idea, Tanner, and Maddie would love it. Of course, we'll watch Amanda. We'd be happy to do it."

Relief rushed through him. If Sherry hadn't been on board, this plan simply wasn't going to happen.

"Do you have any ideas as to where she might like to go? I have a few but I want this to be really special for her. Sort of a birthday trip."

"You know, before I was a stay at home mom, I was an event planner. If you let me, I can help you pull this all together," Sherry offered. "I want her birthday to be something she'll remember forever."

"I wouldn't turn down the help."

"Then we're a team," Sherry laughed. "How about we find a table and I'll eat my snack here while I tell you all the ideas that I have? Maddie's going to love this. I'm thinking warm and tropical. What about you?"

It sounded perfect. It was all coming together.

CHAPTER SEVEN

Tanner had been acting strangely all evening. In a happy and jovial mood, he hadn't ripped anything else apart which was a positive sign. He'd painted the entire living room and tomorrow he was going to put the new baseboards on. That would be a whole project start to finish and she almost found herself cheering out loud.

But there had been something in the way he'd acted, something…different…almost secretive. He'd even left the room to take a call at one point while cooking dinner. He didn't usually do that so she was immediately suspicious. What secrets was her husband keeping from her? Should she ask him what was going on or ignore it? These days she wasn't sure.

"She's asleep finally," Tanner announced, striding into their bedroom and immediately stripping off his shirt. He was still the sexiest man she'd ever seen. "She negotiated for three stories instead of two."

"She's becoming quite the used car salesman. I think we might be spoiling her."

"Naw, it can't hurt to read to her more. If she was asking for cars or jewelry, then we're spoiling her."

"Cars and jewelry?" Maddie giggled. "She's five."

Tanner threw his clothes into the hamper in the closet and climbed into bed wearing his boxers and a t-shirt. Before they'd had Amanda, they'd liked to sleep nude.

"Never too early to ask for her first Porsche."

"Her *first* Porsche? She's going to have multiple Porsches?"

"Not if I have anything to say about it. Now how about you come a little closer?"

Bedroom eyes. She'd heard the phrase in her youth but had never truly known what it meant until she'd met this man. Her heart fluttered in her chest and it suddenly seemed hard to catch her breath. Tanner Marks ought to be illegal in all fifty states.

"How close?"

She'd learned a thing or two since being married to him. He liked to play a little before he got down to business.

"Close. Very close."

Maddie scooted about an inch, but no more.

"This close?"

A slow smile spread across his handsome face. "Aw baby, closer."

This time she set her book on the side table and moved another inch.

"This close?"

He leaned closer and his aroma tickled her nostrils. He smelled amazing, but then he always did. Citrus from his body wash, and she should know. She'd picked it out. But then there was something extra, something more than a simple bottle of soap. It was a warmth she'd never been able to put her finger on but it never ceased to make her think of love, happiness, and home.

"Closer," he invited. "I'll make it worth your while."

Experience told her he was telling the truth.

Maddie scooted even closer until the side of her body was flush with his. The heat from his skin penetrated her own flesh, sending a wash of warmth through her veins all the way to her fingertips.

"I believe you said something about making it worth my while."

She heard the urgency in her own voice but it had always been like this. The want. The aching need that only this one man had ever satisfied. She was sure they would be chasing each other around the house when Amanda was grown and on her own.

Just more slowly.

His fingers slipped under the hem of her t-shirt, brushing her skin and making her tingle all over. "You wear too many clothes to bed."

"I agree but that's what parents do," she reminded him. "Maybe when she's older we can go back to sleeping naked."

His brows arched up and then he swiftly stood, marching over to the bedroom door and flipping the lock.

"Just in case. She was sleeping when I left her room but you never know."

Maddie didn't want to scar her child for life by seeing her parents have sex. She was sure Tanner didn't, either.

Sliding between the sheets, he picked up where he'd left off. Getting her naked.

"I could use a little cooperation here," he whispered, pressing kisses to her neck and partially exposed shoulder. Her pulse skipped a beat and the blood began to roar in her ears. "Lift up a little, babe?"

She complied and her t-shirt slipped over her head and he tossed it over his shoulder so it landed in a puddle on the floor. Her pajama pants quickly followed suit but they still weren't skin to skin.

"Now your clothes are in the way."

He sat up in bed and held out his arms. "Then take them off of me."

"Since when do you let me be in charge?"

"Since now. Unless you don't want to—"

"I do," Maddie replied quickly, before he changed his mind. This was going to be fun. "I'm in charge."

"You're in charge," he repeated but there was mischief twinkling in his blue eyes. "Be gentle. It's my first time."

Snorting, she slid her hands underneath his t-shirt, her hands meeting warm, solid flesh.

"We're a heck of a long way from your first time at anything. Let's just say it's your first time *today*."

"Whatever you want. After all…you're in charge."

Now he was just being a shit.

She tugged at his t-shirt. "Arms up."

Obediently, he lifted his arms, allowing her to pull the t-shirt over his head. Unlike him, however, she didn't toss it on the floor, instead placing it on the nightstand next to the bed. He started to stretch his legs out so she could take off his boxers but she shook her head. She was planning to have a little fun first.

"I'm in charge," she reminded him. "I'll let you know when I'm ready to do that."

His brow quirked but he relaxed back against the pillows without a word. Swinging her leg over his body, she straddled Tanner, resting on the tops of his thighs while her palms glided up his ridged abdomen to his chest and then back down again. He groaned but remained passive under her ministrations, although his jaw tightened slightly.

"I want to play a little bit. And since I'm in charge…"

Leaning down, she began to press kisses along his collarbone, and then dragging her tongue across his salty skin. Tanner groaned and his fingers tightened on her hips but he still didn't say anything or move. Normally she'd be flat on her back by now.

Still taking her time, she languidly dropped kisses on his torso, her head moving in one direction. Down. The muscles on his belly jumped under her lips, and she gave the skin a tiny nibble as she lightly feathered her fingertips over his ribcage and then across the straining material of his boxers. He was hard and ready and it was all she could do not to rip the thin cotton keeping him caged in. Feeling devilish, she rubbed her cheek against the fabric only to hear Tanner grunt and then suddenly found herself flipped over and…

Flat on her back.

Giggling, she held him at bay, her hands against his chest as he hovered over her. "Hey, I was supposed to be in charge."

His smile was playful but a tiny bit evil. "You were and now I am."

"Do I have to do what you say?"

"Of course."

Dipping his head, he lapped at an already hard nipple before pulling it into his mouth, his teeth scraping the sides. Arrows of arousal shot straight to her clit and she moved restlessly underneath him, her fists clenching the sheets. He moved to the other breast while his fingertips traveled down over her abdomen and between her legs.

Pressing two fingers inside of her, he moved them in just the right way to ramp up the pleasure. He knew her body, every single inch, and he'd long ago perfected the art of bringing her to orgasm. His thumb strummed her clit and his other digits stroked the sweet spot inside of her, making her body tremble and her legs shake as her climax took control. White lights sparkled behind her eyes and warmth flooded her veins. She whispered Tanner's name once or twice and then rode those waves as long as she could, stretching out the pleasure for as long as possible. Afterward, she was a puddle of goo in his arms, eyes closed and totally blissed out.

"That looked like fun," Tanner teased, his tongue drawing lazy circles on her shoulder. "Think I might be able to get in on it, too?"

Her lids fluttered open and she ran a fingernail slowly up his arm, his neck, and over his jaw, covered in dark stubble.

"I think that would be an excellent idea."

His hard cock pressed against her thigh and she reached down, taking him in her hand and guided him exactly where she needed him. She was so ready for him that he slid in easily, filling her so deliciously that she couldn't hold back her sigh of pure contentment. Nothing felt better than being this close to her husband. Since becoming parents, they didn't get to do this as often as they'd like but when they did…

Pure heaven.

There was no fumbling or hesitation. They knew each other's rhythms. What made the other moan in pleasure or groan in ecstasy. Sensitive spots like the curve of her neck or behind Tanner's ear. He liked the base of his spine stroked and she loved it when he pounded into her hard and fast, taking her breath away.

Tanner's first few strokes were slow and easy but they quickly built up a fast pace, his body pistoning in and out, every thrust running over that sensitive spot. A bar of arousal built in her belly and her toes curled as another orgasm built to its crescendo. She was teetering on the edge and a puff of wind would send her happily and enthusiastically over. His face was a mask of complete concentration and his jaw tight as he held back his own pleasure.

Reaching between them, Tanner deft fingers circled her clit and she went off like a rocket straight into the stars. Her nails dug into the taut muscles of his shoulders as she careened through the sky, bouncing off clouds. Tanner orgasmed right after, his entire body going stiff and his head thrown back, showing off the cords of his neck.

When it was over they were covered with sticky sweat, their breathing ragged and labored. Maddie's hair was a mess. What wasn't sticking straight up was in tangles around her damp neck. The sheets had half fallen off the bed and at some point, a pillow had gone flying and landed near the bedroom door. She had no memory of that happening but it clearly had.

Life with Tanner Marks was never boring.

Now how did she convince him that they needed a vacation? This might be a good time to do it. He'd be relaxed and in a great mood. She turned to speak to him, levering up so she was leaning on her elbow but the words died before she could say them.

Tanner was asleep, softly snoring, his features almost boyish and relaxed.

Tomorrow. She'd find a time tomorrow and talk to him.

The next evening Tanner could hardly wait for Maddie to arrive home. It was time to spring the big news. He'd had several texts from Sherry this afternoon and it was all set. One week of romance and relaxation, just the two of them.

His wife had always told him how organized her best friend was and how she could create the perfect event, but he hadn't realized how amazing Sherry was. She'd pulled this vacation together in about twenty-four hours and planning trips wasn't even her area of expertise. He could have done it himself but it would have taken much longer.

He and Maddie were going to take a beach vacation.

They'd had friends who had done it and seemed to love everything about it. He had a stack of books he wanted to read and he was excited about getting the time to do it.

"Daddy, why are you standing at the door staring outside?"

How long had he been standing here lost in thought?

"I'm watching for your mom to come home. I have a surprise for her."

Amanda's eyes lit up and her smile widened. "And for me?"

Chuckling, he lifted his daughter into his arms and pressed a kiss to her forehead. "And for you too, but not the same one. How would you like to stay with your Aunt Sherry and Uncle Dan for a few days while Mommy and Daddy go on a little trip?"

She was immediately suspicious. Smart girl. "Can I have ice cream when I'm there?"

"Not for breakfast."

"For 'zert?"

'Zert was Amanda's word for *dessert*. One of the few toddler-years speech affectations that she still used. Tanner would mourn the day when this last one was gone. Maddie was right – their daughter was growing up so fast.

"You can probably have some for dessert but not every single night. More like a treat."

"Aunt Sherry always gives me treats."

That was true. Sherry was a real pushover when it came to sweets while Maddie was stricter, but then she was a doctor.

"Don't expect it all the time," Tanner warned. "So are you happy that you get to stay with Aunt Sherry?"

Amanda nodded. "Where will you and Mommy go?"

"I'm going to take your mom on a vacation to the beach. In Florida."

"Will Mickey Mouse be there?"

Even at five, Amanda knew where Mickey lived.

"I'm positive that he won't be. Is that important?"

"It would be fun to be on vacation with Mickey."

"I can't argue with that. Now when Mommy gets home don't tell her about our surprise, okay? I'll tell her at dinner. Can you keep our secret until then?"

Five-year-olds weren't famous for being able to keep a secret but it would be less than an hour. Amanda could handle that.

"I can do that."

Maddie's car pulled into the driveway and Tanner's heart lurched in his chest. He hadn't had a surprise this big for his wife in a long time.

If you didn't count getting fired. He'd been surprised, too.

He held his finger over his lips. "Okay, Mommy is home so remember. We're going to stay quiet about the surprise, right? Now let's give Mommy a big hug when she comes in the door. She's had a long day."

He placed Amanda's feet on the floor and the little girl flew toward the door as Maddie walked through it, throwing her arms around her mother and giving her a big smack on the cheek.

"Mommy, we're going to the beach and have ice cream!"

Don't trust a five-year-old. He should have known. The cat was officially out of the bag.

Maddie was looking up at him, her eyes round with shock. Good shock or bad shock? At this point, he couldn't tell.

"Surprise. We're going on a second honeymoon."

Ice cream optional.

CHAPTER EIGHT

Maddie wasn't a huge fan of flying and she avoided it as much as practically possible. It wasn't that she was afraid. No, it was the hassle. Get there hours before the flight, wait in several long lines, and then sit around until it was time to leave. Not fun or efficient.

Driving to Florida, however, would have taken way too long so she'd gritted her teeth and dealt with it, happy when the rental car pulled up in front of their lodgings.

"Pretty snazzy, husband," Maddie remarked, stepping out of the car. The warm sun felt absolutely amazing and she couldn't wait to shed the layers of clothing she'd been wearing since Montana. It was a hot day and already she could feel her skin beginning to sizzle. As a redhead, she had to be super careful.

SPF 100 coming right up.

"Sherry did help me," Tanner admitted for the second time. He'd mentioned it before when he'd told her the news and she hadn't been all that surprised. Sherry liked to organize. Cabinets, parties, papers, people; she really wasn't fussy. So of course, when Maddie had agreed that a vacation would be a good idea her friend had moved behind the scenes to make it happen. "She said that we might like having the convenience of a kitchen. We wouldn't have to eat out so much if we didn't want to."

If Maddie were here by herself, eating out would be her only option. That and cereal. She could fix a mean bowl of Cheerios with milk but that was the extent of her culinary skills.

At Sherry's urging, Tanner had rented a luxury condo in a large high-rise instead of a hotel room. Because it was a last-minute booking, it was a sweet deal at a bargain price. She had assured Maddie – more than once – that Tanner wasn't breaking the bank on this vacation. It might look like it but the price was actually quite reasonable, and the condo was more convenient than a hotel. This way they had a kitchen, laundry, and a small balcony overlooking the Gulf of Mexico.

Maddie couldn't wait to sit there and have her morning coffee while watching the waves go in and out. Sweet serenity.

"It's fantastic. You made a great choice. This must be how the other half lives. Wow, this is fancy."

This vacation idea had turned out to be just the thing that her husband had needed to get out of his funk. Once he'd announced it, he'd hurried around the house for the next week trying to finish up all the projects he'd started because he didn't want to come home to chaos. Neither did she and she'd been thrilled.

Gathering up their luggage, they entered the brightly lit lobby, the cool air-conditioning hitting them the moment the door opened. Goosebumps ran up her arm and she shivered slightly. From hot to cold in ten seconds.

The lobby was all marble and chrome, completely modern in design, although they'd painted the walls a turquoise as a concession to the sparkling water outside the doors. On the far wall were two elevators with a set of double doors to the right. A concierge sat at a desk to the left making sure that no one entered that wasn't supposed to be there, although Maddie and Tanner had already had to go through a security gate at the entrance to the parking lot.

The young man at the concierge desk was aware of their arrival and had their keys to the unit along with a short list of rules and regulations for pool usage and such.

"Will you be having any guests here during your stay?" he asked. "If so, they need to check in if they're going to use the pool."

"No guests," Tanner replied. "Just us."

Us. It sounded so wonderful and cozy.

"My name is Brad if you need anything. Restaurant recommendations or tickets to attractions. I'm your guy."

"Thank you, Brad," Maddie said. "That's very helpful."

"Brad knows every decent restaurant all up and down the beaches."

That statement came from an older man, possibly in his late fifties or early sixties. His hair was bleached almost white and his face was dark gold from the sun, making his eyes appear incredibly blue. He was with his wife, a pretty blonde woman that appeared to be at least a few decades younger. They were both dressed for the weather in shorts and t-shirts.

The man held out his hand to Tanner. "I'm Leo Gordon and this is my wife Bibi. We live on fifteen. I'm guessing you're renting out Bill's unit. He's on four."

Brad nodded distractedly, the phone on his desk ringing. "They are renting Bill's. Staying the week."

Leo's already smiling face brightened. "Then you'll have to come for drinks tonight. We can all get to know each other. We won't take no for an answer will we, Bibi?"

Bibi was far more subdued but she also nodded in agreement, extending her hand to Tanner and Maddie.

"It's so nice to meet you."

"It's nice to meet you," Maddie replied. "It's very kind of you to extend an invitation to us."

A little overwhelming too but she didn't want to be rude. It might be nice to meet a few locals.

"Bill always rents to the best people. It's like we get new friends every few weeks," Leo boomed, his voice echoing in the airy lobby. "We love meeting new people, don't we, honey?"

Once again, Bibi nodded. "We do."

She wasn't chatty, that was for sure.

Tanner gave Maddie a look, his brows raised, leaving it all up to her. He wasn't the most social animal and she, of course, had moments of awkwardness with new people but she'd mostly grown out of that by necessity. Before Springwood she'd worked as a doctor in a busy Chicago emergency room, and social anxiety would have been a problem.

Slightly conflicted, Maddie didn't answer immediately. She and Tanner were there for a second honeymoon of sorts and she hadn't expected to socialize much, if at all. However, the couple standing only a few feet away were wearing such expectant and hopeful expressions it would have been terribly rude to say no. It wouldn't hurt to meet a few residents of the building and be friendly. Meeting the neighbors seemed like a good idea. It would probably only be a couple of hours. Tops.

"We'd love to join you," she replied, giving them a warm smile of her own. "Just let us know what time."

"Six o'clock," Leo said, patting his wife's arm affectionately. "It's come as you are, so don't dress up or anything. We'll see you then. Just come to the top floor."

The couple strolled out of the lobby and into the blinding Florida sunshine.

"Interesting couple," Tanner observed. "Are you sure about

having drinks with them? We don't have to if you don't want to."

"I didn't feel pressured. I'm sure it will be fine. We'll spend an hour with them being good neighbors and then we'll be on our own."

Tanner waggled his eyebrows playfully, like a villain in an old silent movie. He was such a goof sometimes. "Just the two of us."

She cast a glance over her shoulder at Brad, who was currently engrossed in a telephone conversation.

"Almost. How about we go upstairs and then call Amanda?"

Then she might try to convince her husband to join her in the shower.

Maddie and Tanner had committed to joining their neighbors for a drink and that was exactly what they were going to do. It was good to be friendly and it wouldn't hurt to spend an hour sipping a cool drink and finding out more about the area.

Already she was far more relaxed than she'd been in a long time. They'd spoken to Amanda and their daughter was having a ball playing with her best friends, watching movies, and eating ice cream. Sherry had assured Maddie that everything was under control so she could simply have a great vacation and leave her worries behind.

Tanner had also visibly relaxed since they'd arrived, the tension that he'd been carrying around his shoulders completely gone. Coming here was a great decision. Maddie was looking forward to sleeping in, reading a few books, eating some good food, and maybe romping in the waves on the beach.

Slathered in sunscreen, of course. She burned easily.

Patting the pocket on his cargo shorts, Tanner closed the

door to their unit behind them.

"I've got the keys. Now what's the signal?"

She slipped her hand into his. "Signal?"

"You know…for when we're ready to leave. Tap your nose? Run your fingers through your hair?"

He was being silly and she loved it. He hadn't been this laid back since he'd lost his job.

"How about I just tell you that I'm ready to leave? Is that too straightforward?"

"That sounds good in theory but what if they're the type that never wants anyone to leave?"

"Then I'll tap my nose. Ready?"

"Let's do this."

They took the elevator to fifteen, which was the top, and stepped out into the hallway. There was only one door so it had to belong to Leo and Bibi. They had the entire floor.

"Looks like they have the penthouse suite," Tanner observed. "The place must be huge."

Tanner knocked firmly a few times and they only waited a few seconds before the door swung open and a grinning Leo stood there, cocktail in hand.

"You made it. Excellent. Come on in. What's your poison?"

They'd already talked about this. Since Tanner didn't drink – and hadn't for years – it was often simpler if Maddie had a glass of wine and he would explain that he couldn't have alcohol because of some medication he was on. These weren't friends and he didn't feel like explaining his drinking history with people he'd only just met. For some reason, if both he and Maddie didn't drink people seemed a hell of a lot more upset than when only he didn't. He didn't know why but he'd seen it over the years.

"Water or soda for me," Tanner replied as Maddie perused

the bottles Leo had placed on the kitchen counter. They were well-stocked. "Maddie wouldn't mind a glass of white wine."

Leo grabbed a glass and began playing bartender. "Are you on the wagon?"

"Sadly, I'm on a medication that doesn't play well with alcohol."

Chuckling, Leo handed Maddie her wine and then reached for a can of ginger ale. "That's too bad. I make a mean rum runner. I don't suppose I can talk you into it, Maddie?"

She wasn't sure what a rum runner was but from the name it had to have rum in it. The last time she'd had a rum drink she'd ended up with a king-sized headache the next day. She'd stick to white wine or perhaps vodka.

"I'm pacing myself tonight. I'll stay with the wine." She took a sip. Fruity. "This is very nice."

"It's from a vineyard in Williamsburg, Virginia," Bibi said, appearing from a doorway off the living room. "We visited on vacation. The white is especially good."

"It's wonderful." Maddie took another sip. Now that she had had a chance to look around the apartment, she realized that they weren't the only guests. There were others as well. "Really nice. I don't drink much, actually, but this is good."

A tall brunette stood from her perch on a kitchen barstool and held out her hand. "It's one of my favorites too whenever Leo and Bibi invite me over. I'm Ashley, by the way. Ashley Monroe. I'm in unit E on eight. Welcome to the neighborhood, even if it's only for a week or so."

Ashley was gorgeous. The kind of beauty that looked effortless and elegant. Golden skin, luxuriant hair, and a great body. Tonight she was wearing a bright red sundress that would have made Maddie look like a ghost.

"It's nice to meet you," Tanner said. "And thank you for the welcome. We are staying only one week."

A large, muscular man with sandy blond hair shot with gray that had been standing near the open sliding glass doors to the balcony joined the group. "Where y'all from?"

"Springwood, Montana," Tanner replied. "I'm–"

He broke off and Maddie knew why. He'd been about to say that he was the sheriff there but he couldn't say that anymore.

Damn that pissant mayor.

"I'm happy to be in some warmer weather," Tanner finally said, amending his statement.

"Me too," Maddie said, giving Tanner a smile. "It's already winter back home."

The man's name turned out to be Randy Knight, ex-football player who now owned a chain of pizza parlors after blowing out his knee catching a winning touchdown pass. He and his wife Carrie – who had shown up a few minutes later – lived in the unit next to Ashley.

Everyone was quite friendly and the conversation – and drinks – flowed. They all seemed fascinated that Maddie was a real, live, actual doctor. After more than one question about what he did, Tanner admitted that he was a former sheriff in their hometown but didn't give any details. Luckily, the group seemed to assume that he'd retired early. She'd showed them pictures of Amanda and they had produced photos of their own, some of kids, some of dogs, and Randy showed off a picture of his boat which he had named *Cute Carrie*.

They shared their opinions about the best beaches and restaurants, but it was when Maddie was alone with Ashley that they began to share their opinions about each other. Maddie had gone out onto the balcony to look at the view and the woman joined her, leaning on the railing and staring out onto the emerald green water.

"How long have you been married?" Ashley asked. "If you don't mind my saying, you look a little younger than your husband."

She wasn't the first person to notice but most people didn't remark on it.

"We've been married almost ten years," Maddie replied. "And yes, Tanner is older but that's never bothered me."

Ashley glanced over her shoulder where Tanner, Leo, and Randy were talking inside.

"It wouldn't bother me, either. He's a good-looking son of a gun, isn't he?"

Maddie wasn't a jealous person by nature but she wasn't sure she liked how Ashley stared at her husband. Sort of…hungry.

"I think so."

"Leo and Bibi are good people, and so are Randy and Carrie, for that matter. They're fun and easy to be around. You might want to give Leo a wide berth, though. He likes the ladies and you're very attractive." She glanced over her shoulder again. "Although your husband might beat Leo into the ground if he looked at you wrong. I don't think most men would want to tangle with him. He said he was a cop, right?"

Not sure what to say, Maddie stalled by taking another sip of her wine that had gone warm. She'd been nursing the glass for over half an hour.

"He was a sheriff. What is it that you do, Ashley?"

The woman's smile widened. "I don't really do anything. I'm divorced and my ex had money."

Oh.

"Does my candor bother you?" Ashley asked, chuckling. "I married for money and I don't deny it. I'll probably do it again before I lose my looks."

Okey-dokey.

"You married for love," Ashley said. "It's okay if you want to judge me. Lots of people do."

Having been on the wrong side of people's judgments in her youth, Maddie didn't want to be that kind of person. So far Ashley hadn't been anything but up front and honest.

"I don't want to judge you, and yes, I married for love."

"I might do that someday. Crazier things have happened." There was a crash in the kitchen and both women turned around. Carrie had dropped a glass on the tile floor and it had shattered into a million little pieces. "Looks like Carrie has had a few too many. Again. She's been drinking more and more since Randy took up with Bibi."

Maddie and Tanner had been at this cocktail hour less than forty-five minutes and it had become like the story line of a bad soap opera.

A gold digger. And now the husband of one couple cheating with the wife of another.

Ashley leaned down closer to Maddie, whispering in her ear. "Don't feel too badly for Leo. He was planning on trading up wives soon, anyway. Bibi's number three and turned thirty-five last year. Leo likes them young, and she would know. She was his assistant fresh out of college when he found her and left number two."

Yep, bad soap opera all around. All they'd been trying to do was be friendly with the neighbors. That's it. One drink and they were out. Maddie didn't really want to get pulled into the local drama. She'd simply wanted to be sociable. Now she wanted to make as graceful an exit as possible. Preferably soon.

Catching her husband's eye, she turned slightly away from Ashley, ducked her head down, and then as slyly as possible…

Tapped her nose.

✧ ✧ ✧ ✧

"She did not say that," Tanner said, shaking his head. He and Maddie were sitting in a lovely beachside restaurant eating a late dinner as the sky turned purple, orange, and pink. "Why on earth would she tell you that?"

His wife had just recounted her conversation with Ashley Monroe and he'd been floored by the woman's candor. If she was telling the truth, of course.

"Maybe she was pulling your leg," Tanner suggested. "Playing a joke on the hicks from a little town in Montana. Hell, for all we know, she does this with everyone that rents that condo. Perhaps it's a game the whole group plays."

"That would be a strange and sick game. She seemed perfectly serious." Maddie's brow quirked. "And she seemed especially enamored of you."

Ashley Monroe didn't interest him in the least.

"I'm a one-woman man, baby. You know that."

"I do, which is why I'm not worried. About you. But she said that I might want to give Leo a wide berth and I suggest you do the same with her. While I trust you with my life, I don't trust her."

Tanner felt the same about their host. Leo had also made a remark about how attractive Maddie was and that Tanner was a lucky man. Randy, on the other hand, had been far more discreet. Now Maddie was telling him the guy was having an affair with their host's wife.

"Did you see anything between Randy and Bibi?" Maddie asked. "You were with them more than I was."

He didn't remember the two of them even speaking to each other once.

"Bibi stayed in the background. I mostly talked to Randy and Leo."

"What about?"

"Sports, mostly. Randy used to be a pro football player before he messed up his knee. We also talked about boats, which I know nothing about, and decent restaurants within walking distance. That's how we got here."

Wrinkling her nose, Maddie rolled her eyes. "Sports. The universal language between men."

"Come on, now. You like sports, too."

"Yes, but it's not the first thing that I talk about when I meet people."

"Not for me either, but it made sense since Randy was an athlete." He reached across the table and captured her hand with his. "Listen, we did the polite thing and went to their cocktail party. Now we can go on with the rest of our vacation. If they invite us again, we can just tell them that we already have plans."

"It wasn't that I hated them or anything. I actually kind of liked Ashley, but we came on vacation to have some time with each other."

Maddie didn't hate anyone. Even when she probably should.

"That's true. Now that we're done with dinner, how about you and me taking a walk on the beach in the moonlight? Just the two of us."

She gave him a playful smile. "That sounds like an excellent idea."

Tanner wasn't a twenty-year-old anymore but damned if this woman didn't make him feel that way. He'd never get tired of being with her.

After paying the check, he took her hand and led her down a wooden staircase to the soft sand below. It was completely dark out now, the sun asleep until morning, but it was far from dark. Along with the sliver of moon over head, the condos were a wall of lights, each window a lamp casting shadows at their feet.

They'd kicked off their shoes and let the cool waves lap at

their toes, dancing around when the water got too close. There were a few other people out and about but for the most part it was quiet and peaceful. A state that Tanner hadn't had nearly enough of lately.

"We should have done this years ago."

Maddie laughed, the sound mixing with the waves and the soft wind. "How? You could barely get four days off in a row. And now that you've been let go, the town wants Pete's head on a platter. Sherry sent me a text earlier today that he's begun to hide and won't go out in public. There are rumors he's left town, escaped in the night like a criminal."

Tanner had received the same messages from Sam, his former deputy. Somehow the thought of Pete cowering in his big house on the hill didn't make him feel any better. Springwood was in chaos and the duly elected mayor was hiding.

"Pete didn't think it all the way through. He just wanted the budget cuts."

Maddie paused, turning toward him. Even in the dim light he could see the indecision in her expression, which surprised him. It wasn't like her to wonder whether she should say something.

"What's on your mind, Maddie?"

"If Pete offered you your job back, would you take it?"

Funny, he'd been pondering that very question. With all the texts he'd been receiving since they'd left home, it appeared that the town was in a full-blown mutiny. Hiding might have been the first wise action Pete had ever made.

"I don't know," he finally replied. Because he didn't know for sure. He had pride but sitting around wasn't his style, either. "I'd love to tell Pete where to shove his sheriff's position, but then I think about the town and I know that I can do a good job. Hell, it's all I know how to do. It's what I am."

"It's not all you are."

Her words were spoken so softly he'd almost not heard.

"A man defines himself but what he does, honey, and how he takes care of the people he loves."

She'd been looking down but now her head came up, her gaze searching his face. For what? He wasn't sure.

"You're more than the sheriff of Springwood, Tanner Marks. And you take care of us just fine."

Snorting, he shook his head. "Letting you pay all the bills? I don't think so."

"Is that what this is about? Money? If the roles were switched—"

"But they're not," he interjected smoothly. "You knew I was an old-fashioned man when you married me."

"Stubborn, too," she muttered. "You make a mule look reasonable."

"You love me anyway."

Her smile widened and she stepped closer, placing her palms on his chest. The heat from her skin seared him through the thin cotton of his t-shirt and his stomach clenched. He loved this woman more than he could even begin to express.

"I do love you." Her hand slid up to his shoulder and she stood on her tiptoes to kiss him, but then her attention was quickly pulled away. Her brow was wrinkled and pinched together. "Is that Bibi?"

Turning around, Tanner watched Bibi and another man that he couldn't identify disappear into the back door of a condo building just down from their own.

It didn't look like Leo.

"Yes, that's Bibi."

"That wasn't Leo, was it?"

"It could have been Leo. I didn't get a good look."

"Neither did I, but he seemed too tall to be Leo. He kind of looked like…Randy."

"Maybe they're just visiting friends."

Even to his own ears the excuse sounded lame.

"You're right. That's probably what it was. Just a visit to friends."

It could be completely innocent. Or not. He didn't really care or want to get involved. In a week, he'd never see any of them ever again.

Tanner hadn't had a great feeling about the people they'd met tonight to begin with and this confirmed it. Not only was Maddie going to take Ashley's advice, Tanner was going to do it as well.

Give Leo Gordon – and all of his friends – a wide berth.

CHAPTER NINE

For the first time in months, Tanner didn't wake up before
Maddie. When the rich aroma of coffee tickled his nostrils
the next morning and he opened his eyes, his wife's side of the
bed was empty.

He'd slept in.

A bit. It wasn't late, the sun barely up. But considering that
he'd been awake before dawn every day for months this was a
major victory. He didn't know how he'd won the battle but he
could only hope that the war would be next.

Levering out of bed, he pulled on a pair of cargo shorts and
a t-shirt and padded on bare feet out to the kitchen where
Maddie had made a pot of coffee. She couldn't cook at all but
she made a damn fine cup of coffee. He poured himself a mug,
inhaling the delicious smell that was slowly waking him up.

Maddie had taken the newspaper out to the balcony to drink
her coffee and was currently wearing an old pair of sweats, her
feet propped up on a chair. The sun was rising slowly making a
golden halo around her fiery hair, like a mixture of devil and
angel.

He leaned down to give her a kiss good morning. "I don't

suppose you'd share some of that newspaper with me? And where did you get it to begin with?"

"I got up early to see the sunrise and then remembered that the condo is facing west. Then I heard the thump of the delivery person against the door, and I peeked out and there was a newspaper on the mat." She pulled out a section and placed it on the table. "You can have sports. I'm keeping comics."

Settling into the chair opposite, Tanner stretched out his legs and took in the sunrise spread out before him. Maddie had been talking about doing this the entire trip here and she was right. It was a terrific way to start the day.

"Beautiful, isn't it?" she said with a sigh, sipping her coffee. "It's the same sky that we have at home but somehow it's just amazing."

"That's because we don't have to hurry and get to work right after we see it. We can sit here and enjoy it."

"You're so practical."

"You're so romantic."

Maddie liked to pretend that she was all efficient and practical, the professional physician, but as he'd grown to know her more deeply, he'd learned that she was quite fanciful at times. Watching her play dolls, unicorns, and princesses with their daughter never ceased to bring a lump to this throat. There were so many facets to her that he found fascinating.

But his Maddie wasn't having any of it. "I am not a romantic."

"You are. You definitely are. Just admit it."

She playfully stuck out her tongue. "I won't admit anything."

He waggled his brows. "I could make you admit it."

"Promises, promises."

"You ought to know by now, Maddie, that I'm a man that keeps my word."

His wife didn't have the opportunity to reply. A scream ripped through the air from down on the beach. Both he and Maddie flew to the railing and looked down. A woman and man walking their dog were bent over a prone figure on the sand, the water lapping at the still limbs of the person.

Something bad had happened last night.

Bibi Gordon was dead.

It appeared that she'd been strangled with her own scarf and left on the beach sometime during the night to be discovered when the sun came up. Tanner and Maddie, along with the couple that had found the body had waited until the police arrived, of course, but now a large crowd had gathered to see what the fuss was about.

At some point, someone must have alerted Leo because he was talking to one of the cops. Red-faced and crying, he kept shaking his head and asking who would do such a thing. As a former law enforcement officer, Tanner could have answered that question.

A hell of a lot of people, sadly. There were too many sick and twisted individuals in this world. A lot of good people too, but the bad apples made it difficult for everybody.

The officer finally finished with Leo and wanted to speak with Tanner and Maddie since they'd been on the scene almost from the beginning.

"I'm Sheriff Ken Smith," the man said, shaking their hands. He didn't look old enough to be a sheriff, maybe in his mid-thirties, but then Tanner remembered he'd been about that age when he'd taken over Springwood. This little beach town was even smaller. "Can I ask you folks a few questions?"

The sheriff had pulled them aside while the coroner was

dealing with Bibi's body.

"First of all, can I get your names?"

Tanner placed his arm around Maddie's shoulders. "My name is Tanner Marks and this is my wife Dr. Madison Shay Marks. We're from Springwood, Montana and on vacation here. We're renting a condo in the same building as the Gordons."

He'd told more than their names but Tanner knew what questions were coming next, so he might as well get it all out there.

The sheriff wrote the information into a notebook, the pencil scratching on the paper. "Tanner Marks from– Wait, Tanner Marks? *The* Tanner Marks? The one who helped bring in Wade Bryson, the serial killer?"

Maddie stiffened next to him. He'd never get used to this. When he and his friends had put an end to Bryson's reign of death and destruction there had been a great deal of press coverage. Too much, in Tanner's opinion. All of them had received a shit load of notoriety and none of it was wanted. All he'd been doing was helping a friend. That was it. He didn't do it for the glory or to get his name in the papers and magazines. He'd been there for Logan. They'd succeeded. Now everyone knew his damn name.

"Yes," Maddie replied softly. "My husband helped stop Wade Bryson."

She'd told him she was proud of him. She'd told him that before he'd even left to do the job and then again when he'd come back alive. She'd never once complained about the dangerous situations his job put him in, nor had she complained when he'd gone to help Logan. She could have, but that wasn't her style.

Sheriff Ken Smith's eyes were wide and his mouth had fallen open in surprise. Eventually he pulled himself together and a huge grin spread across his face.

"Holy cow, Tanner Marks. In my little town. Wow, I never thought I'd meet someone like you. You and your friends are amazing. I'd love to hear some stories–"

"Did you have more questions for us?" Tanner cut in. He didn't want to tell any stories of glory and fame.

The sheriff cleared his throat and nodded. "Ah yes, I do. Uh...so you found the body along with the other couple?"

"Technically, they found the body. We were sitting on our balcony having coffee and we heard one of them scream. We looked over the railing and saw someone lying on the sand. We went downstairs to see if we could help–"

"Because you're a trained first responder," Smith interjected helpfully. "That makes sense."

That hadn't even crossed Tanner's mind when he'd run downstairs. It had simply been an instinct.

"We found Bibi with a scarf wrapped around her neck and she was clearly dead."

It hadn't been a pretty sight, either. Luckily, Maddie was a doctor and had a cast iron stomach.

"Did you see anyone around? Anyone suspicious?"

Huh?

"The beach was pretty much deserted."

This wasn't his murder to worry about.

He should just leave it alone.

But this guy was in over his head.

"I doubt the murderer would stick around," Tanner said. "I think she'd been dead for awhile."

Smith frowned. "What makes you say that?"

"Because she was already in rigor. That sets in anywhere between three and six hours after death, so the killer was probably long gone before she was discovered."

"Right. That's right." Smith nodded, scratching more down in his notebook. "Three to six hours. Right."

Dammit.

"Son, is this your first murder case?"

Tanner kept his voice down so that no one else could hear but the three of them.

Smith's gaze darted left and then right and then back to Tanner. "Uh, yes. Does it show? I've been on the job for less than a year and apparently the last murder around here was five years ago."

It showed.

"Less than a year?" Tanner queried. "How long were you a deputy?"

The sheriff shook his head. "The job is an elected position. I got laid off from my computer programming job and thought I'd give it a shot. I've always liked to read about crime and serial killers. I won by thirty votes."

Holy shit.

"You've never been to the academy or studied law enforcement?"

Smith scratched his chin. "I read the manual. Honestly, until today this was the easiest job I've ever had. Nothing ever happens here."

Until it does. Then the citizens were up shit creek without the proverbial paddle. Whoever the killer was, he wasn't stupid. He had to know that the local police were inexperienced and the chances were slim that he'd be caught.

Ken Smith was smiling again. "Wait...why don't you help? You're like...one of the greatest sheriffs ever, right? You can teach me."

No. No...just...no.

Tanner couldn't think of anything he wanted to do less. A

root canal? Major surgery? Those would be higher on the list than trying to train some IT guy on how to be a cop. He'd done it in the past and he'd more than satisfied the karma gods.

Maddie's own eyes had gone wide and she looked horrified at the thought that he might say yes. He'd find a nice way to tell this young sheriff that he wasn't giving up his second honeymoon to chase a killer.

"About that…I'm really sorry but I'm no longer in law enforcement. I guess you could say that I'm retired. My wife and I are here on vacation as well. I'm sure you'll do fine." Tanner glanced over his shoulder to the condo buildings behind him. He could at least head the man in the right direction. "The first thing I'd do is check for security cameras. One might have captured footage of the crime or persons of interest. Maybe a witness or two. Then make up a chart of the crime scene, showing where everyone was at the time of death. You'll need the medical examiner to tell you that. I don't suppose you have any forensics in this town?"

Smith's smile fell and he shook his head. "For a crime scene, I think I'm supposed to call the county or state, but I'm not sure."

"Call one of them. They'll for sure tell you if they're not who is supposed to help. But get one of them here and in the meantime get your deputies to secure the crime scene until they can arrive. Depending on how busy they are, it could be several hours."

Wincing, Smith rubbed the back of his neck. "Yeah…there's only three of us and Deke is on vacation. I'm supposed to have a fourth position but no one has applied for the job because it doesn't pay very much."

Shit.

"Let me guess," Tanner replied grimly. "Budget cuts?"

Smith nodded. "I suppose I could get Deke out of bed. He's got a few days off but I don't think he went anywhere."

"Get him in uniform and get him out here," Tanner growled. "It's all hands on deck when there's been a murder. You can always call in the county or state if your team can't handle it. In fact, that might be the best thing you could do."

"Then I won't get elected again," Tanner heard Ken Smith mutter under his breath.

That might be for the best.

Tanner gave the novice lawman a hard look. "Someone was killed here last night. Someone is dead, Sheriff. That trumps your election or your deputy's vacation. In fact, it trumps it all – sleep, food, fun. A human being was murdered and it's your responsibility to find out who did it. This isn't a movie or video game. This is real life and this poor woman is depending on you for justice."

Sheriff Ken Smith's skin had turned a peculiar shade of green and he looked like he wanted to puke.

"I don't know if I can do this."

"I said the same thing on my first murder case."

Tanner had been that nervous but, dammit, at least he'd had training.

"And you caught the guy?" Smith sounded hopeful again, like maybe all of this was going to be okay. "You solved it, right?"

It was so long ago Tanner barely remembered. It was vague but it was there.

"I did. Two friends got in an argument. One ended up dead. I talked to the friend and he eventually confessed after awhile. It was a long time ago."

"Someone might confess."

"They could. I wouldn't count on it, though."

"But it's possible?"

"Yes, anything is possible. But not probable."

"It would be great if someone would confess."

From the looks of the crowd gathered, it didn't look to Tanner that anyone was anxious to do that. Sighing, he shot his wife a look of apology.

"Listen, if you need any advice that would be okay. I'm staying in that building there in 4A. We'll be in and out but you can always leave me a note or something."

Ken Smith grinned from ear to ear. "That would be awesome. Just great. Thanks, man. I really appreciate it. I really, really do."

Christ, now Tanner felt terrible about not helping even more.

"I also need to tell you that my wife and I were out for a walk last night on the beach and we saw Bibi going into that gray building down the way with a man. From where we were standing, we couldn't see who it was but it didn't look like her husband."

Smith rapidly scratched down the information. "Wow, okay. That's good. You don't know who it was?"

Maddie shook her head. "It was too dark. But he was tall. Bibi only came up to his shoulder."

Tanner nodded in agreement. "He was wearing light-colored pants and a dark t-shirt. It looked like he maybe had light brown hair but once again it was hard to see in the dark. That's why you need to get the surveillance footage. One of those security cameras might have got a better look at him. You want talk to whoever he is as soon as possible."

"Right. Got it. Thanks. I guess I better call Deke."

The sheriff ambled off, phone to his ear, the lone deputy on his heels. What a clusterfuck.

"That was nice of you."

Maddie didn't sound mad but then she rarely lost her temper, despite being a true redhead. She'd always defied the stereotype of a redhead with a nasty temper. She was usually quite laid back.

"Are you mad? I don't want to ruin our vacation but dammit, he isn't–"

"It's fine," she assured him. "You're right. That poor man is in over his head and Bibi deserves justice. You helping him might be her only hope."

"I'm not helping him," Tanner denied. "I'm just…advising. Hell, it's not even consulting. He ought to just call in the state police. They'd probably be happy to take over the investigation. He can learn from them."

Her head tilted to the side, her gaze steady on him. "Usually you'd be all over a case like this."

"Usually it would be my responsibility. It's not. Plus, we're here on vacation. This is supposed to be our second honeymoon. Are you getting tired of me already? It's only been two days," he joked.

"Not in the least, but if you want to do this, I wouldn't stop you."

Did he want to do this? The instinctual part of him was raring to go. It was a case and he wanted to be all on top of it.

But this wasn't Springwood and he wasn't the sheriff here. It wasn't his to solve.

I'm not a sheriff anymore.

But there was another part of him that didn't want to go backwards. In some ways in the last few weeks he'd crossed over inside. Law enforcement was good but he'd been saying over and over for years that he was getting too damn old. He loved helping people but there had to be another way besides getting the crap beat out of him as sheriff of a small town. He just didn't know what "it" was.

"I'm fine in a consulting capacity. I think if we point the sheriff in the right direction he'll do okay."

Maddie didn't look convinced. "If you think so…"

"He'll be fine. How difficult could it be? This town is so small there's probably less than half a dozen real, honest to god suspects."

Maddie's gaze wandered across the sand to where Leo was now talking to the newly arrived Randy, Carrie, and a crying Ashley.

If this were his case? His number one suspect would be Leo Gordon. Just where had he been last night? And who was the man with Bibi?

CHAPTER TEN

Maddie was sitting on the beach later that morning when Ashley joined her, pointing at the empty lounge chair that Tanner had left behind when he went upstairs to make a phone call.

"Do you have a moment?"

"Sure," Maddie replied, setting her book aside. "Have a seat."

Ashley's gaze rested on Maddie's enormous straw hat. "Do you not like the sun?"

"I love the sun but sometimes it doesn't like me. I need to be careful."

Settling on the chair, Ashley crossed her long legs. Today she was wearing a pair of white shorts and a pink tank top. She appeared far more composed than she had this morning. "I wanted to let you know that Leo has decided to have a get together for Bibi tonight. Sort of a celebration of life. I've been helping him with the preparations. He'd love for you and your husband to attend if you can. Seven o'clock. There will be a lot of people there. Bibi was well-loved in this town."

"Tonight?"

That's…fast.

"Bibi had always been very clear about her wishes, apparently. She didn't want a formal funeral and all that fuss. She wanted a party and then to be cremated, her ashes sprinkled in the Gulf. So Leo is making sure she gets what she wants…wanted. No sense delaying it. It only drags out the inevitable."

"I'll talk to Tanner about it," Maddie replied, deliberately noncommittal. Their conversation last night had been about spending more time together than with their temporary neighbors.

Ashley stood, seemingly happy with Maddie's response. "Seven o'clock. See you then."

Waving, the woman walked down the beach, talking to a few people on her way. Tanner returned a few minutes later, lying back in his chair. He had two cold drinks and handed her one.

"Ashley stopped by. She invited us to Bibi's wake."

"We're leaving on Saturday so I doubt we'll be here."

Au contraire.

"It's tonight."

His brows shot up. "Tonight? That's—"

"Fast," Maddie finished for him. "That's exactly what I was thinking. Apparently, Bibi had always been clear about her wishes and she didn't want a funeral. Just a party and to be cremated."

She'd been thinking about this for the last five minutes and it wasn't adding up.

"You seem really angry about that," Tanner said, his tone cautious. "Are your cheeks red from the sun or are you pissed off? Because whatever I did, I'm sorry and I didn't mean to."

She gave her husband a sour look. "Don't do that. Don't act like you're some pussy whipped husband who tiptoes around his wife because we both know you're about as far from that as one human being can get. And no, it's not the sun. I'm wearing sunscreen and a hat, plus I have this sun umbrella. I'm not getting a sunburn this vacation."

Tanner was laughing at her, his shoulders shaking and his lips turned up. He was trying to pretend he wasn't but he was a terrible actor.

"Did I say something funny?"

"Yes," he replied honestly. "But I'm mostly laughing at the situation, not you specifically."

"Right. Care to tell me why you're so damn amused, husband?"

Grinning, Tanner chuckled. "Well…wife, hearing you say the words *pussy whipped* is pretty damn funny."

"Is that it?"

"No," Tanner said with a shake of his head. "And I agree that I'm not henpecked. What I am is wise. Or at least I hope I am. It's not worth starting an argument when I don't want to fight with you. It's our vacation and I want us to have fun."

"Henpecked," Maddie muttered. "I hate that phrase."

"You really do have a bee in your bonnet. What's going on?"

She should let this drop. She really should. But…

"Let me ask you a question. Have we ever in all of our years together talked about what kind of funeral we want or how we should handle death? Because I don't think we have."

Leaning back in the chair, Tanner strummed his lower lip for a moment. "We did have a will drawn up. That's about death."

"But we didn't talk about funerals. We talked about money and bank accounts, and the deed to the house. We talked about Sherry raising Amanda if something happened to both of us. We didn't talk about burial versus cremation."

"To be fair, that's kind of morbid. It was bad enough talking about what we did. That was the most fucking depressing appointment with a lawyer I've ever had and I've been divorced. That's saying something."

It had been a somber occasion but they'd both known that it needed to be done.

"Do you want to be cremated?"

That question had her husband sitting up straight, his legs straddling the chair. "Do whatever you want. I'll be dead and I won't care. Honestly, honey, I try not to think about death too much. It's bad enough that I'm older than you and will probably go years earlier. Maybe I'm a little superstitious but planning my funeral feels like inviting death in for tea and offering him a cookie. Do you think about death much?"

Did she? Not until lately. And it wasn't so much death as just feeling *older* and wishing that she could freeze time.

Wait…that's just a roundabout way of thinking about it.

"I wouldn't say that I dwell on it," she finally replied. "But we're not getting any younger, are we?"

Her husband was looking at her like he'd never seen her before in his life.

"Since when do you worry about getting older? You're young, Maddie. You've got many, many years ahead of you."

"You think that I'm young because you're older, but I'm not that young. I'm going to be forty-one on Friday."

Her thirties had flown by so quickly they were a blur, and people always said that life sped up as a person aged. If that was true, she was going to get whiplash from her forties.

"You're still young."

Bless her husband. He would always say that.

"I am still young," she conceded. "But I'm not *as young* as I once was."

"None of us are."

He didn't get it.

"I don't think we're getting anywhere here. The reason I brought up the subject was that I found it strange that Leo and Bibi had talked funerals, that's all. I didn't intend to start a philosophical discussion about death, aging, and the meaning of the word old."

Tanner swung his leg over the lounge chair so he was now facing her directly.

"Maddie, tell me what's bothering you."

She'd happily answer that question but she didn't even know herself. So she ducked the question.

"I just find it suspicious that Leo Gordon is having this celebration of life party less than twenty-four hours after her death. He's having her cremated, too. And that inexperienced sheriff is probably going to let him."

"You think Leo had something to do with his wife's untimely demise?"

She wasn't the cop in the family but she didn't think she needed a badge to be able to see that Leo Gordon was acting suspiciously.

"Let's just say that I wonder when Leo started making these party plans. Did he call the caterer last week?"

She sounded frustrated because she was.

"That's a good question."

"A question Sheriff Ken Smith probably doesn't know to find the answer to."

"You sound like you think I should get involved with this case."

Tanner did this sometimes. His expression would go bland and he'd make even blander statements as he waited for her to get to the point. The problem was she wasn't sure what the damn point of all of this was. She didn't even know why she was irritated. Tanner hadn't done anything to deserve this except sit down next to her.

"I'm not saying that. All I'm saying is that his behavior raises my suspicions and I'm not even a cop."

"Then it should raise the sheriff's as well," Tanner replied. "Leo Gordon might very well want to cremate his wife as quickly as possible but he has to wait until the medical examiner finishes the autopsy. He can't speed that process up, and if this little town is anything like Springwood he's going to have to wait awhile. He can throw his party as soon as he wants but some of this is out of his control."

"I don't really want to go to that party," she blurted out before she could stop herself. "We probably should go, but I don't really want to. I'm not even sure I like those people. Ashley was nice but I got a weird vibe from all of them, to be honest."

If her husband was surprised, he didn't bat an eyelash at her declaration, simply nodding in agreement.

"That's fine. We only met them once for a few hours, after all. If we don't go, I doubt anyone would notice. If you want, we can walk to that drugstore a few blocks down and pick him up a sympathy card. We can send our condolences that way."

He was doing it again. Wearing that blank expression.

"You think I'm a terrible person, right? You think I'm awful?"

His smile was slow but sweet. "Honey, I think you're the most amazing person I've ever known. I get why you don't want to go. The whole group was a little too soap opera drama for me, but for the most part they seemed like nice people."

"One of those people might be a killer," Maddie pointed out. She couldn't get that out of her head.

"It's a possibility. Cops usually look at the spouse first, statistically speaking."

"It could have been Randy that she was with last night."

"Or someone else. We don't really know. Hopefully it was captured on a security camera. They're everywhere these days. We do know that the security guard has one at the gate. If the killer came in that way, then there's a record of it."

"If I were a killer, I wouldn't come in that way. That would be stupid."

Tanner's smile grew wider. "Okay, honey. How would you do it?"

She'd given that question some thought this morning.

"If I didn't already live in the building, I'd park somewhere else and walk here on the beach."

"You might be captured on cameras," Tanner said.

"Yes, but I might be able to stay in the shadows."

"That's true. Then what?"

"I'd lure Bibi outside. I'd call her and have her meet me somewhere on the beach that was dark and deserted."

"Then you're assuming that she was killed by someone she knew?"

Was she? Yes.

"I am," Maddie confirmed. "You're always saying that stranger murders are uncommon."

"It's nice to know that you've been listening. Then what?"

"Well…then I'd strangle her, I guess."

"With her own scarf? You didn't bring anything with you? That's not good planning."

"You're saying that the murder may not have been premeditated?"

He shrugged carelessly. "I'd vote for a crime of passion."

She nudged his leg with her bare foot. "So…talk. How do you think it happened?"

"They used her own scarf. That leads me to believe that it was a crime of passion or opportunity. Now, I could be wrong.

They may have brought a weapon with them but ended up using a more convenient one, but if I had a gun or a knife, I would use those items first."

He levered to his feet and beckoned to her, turning her so that she stood facing the condo buildings, her back to the water.

"Now tell me what you see."

She wasn't sure what he was getting at.

"It's a building, Tanner."

He shook his head. "No, really look at it. Look at all of those windows on our building and the two next to us. You know what those are? Possible witnesses. When we were talking last night, I noticed that it wasn't unusual for people to leave their drapes open. With a great view like that it's not a surprise. I don't know about you but if I were planning to murder some-one, I wouldn't do it in full view of several condo buildings. Even in the middle of the night, someone might have seen."

"That's why you don't think it was premeditated."

"It could be. I just think it's more likely that Bibi and whom-ever she was with argued and it got heated and she ended up dead. Hell, for all I know, she was out here alone and was killed for her wedding ring or something. It's not common but it could happen. Even in this little town. But if I were planning to kill my wife? I wouldn't do it here."

They'd gone in a circle and were back where they started.

"Every time we answer a question all we get are more ques-tions."

"Welcome to policework, honey. It's frustrating as hell."

That was an understatement. No wonder Tanner wasn't anxious to jump into the middle of this case. Maybe it was better that they keep their distance. They'd get Leo a nice sympathy card and give him a wide berth. This was their vacation and they didn't need to get mixed up in a murder.

Even if one of their neighbors was a killer.

CHAPTER ELEVEN

For some reason Tanner didn't want to admit to Maddie, he'd already called in a few favors from his law enforcement buddies.

In other words, he wasn't as uninterested in this case as he outwardly appeared.

It certainly wasn't because it was interesting and unique. Sadly, murder between husbands and wives was all too common… If that's what this was.

It was more that he needed the challenge. He'd managed to keep his body busy since he'd been fired but his mind was begging him to try and solve this case. Because he was fucking bored. Retirement sounded like hell right about now.

He didn't play golf, or hang around the coffee shop. He didn't do woodworking and he hadn't gone fishing in a damn long time. He was a lousy candidate for rest and relaxation. At least his brain was. His beaten and battered body might want to weigh in on this discussion too, with an entirely different opinion. But in the meantime, here he was returning a phone call from his best friend Logan Wright regarding any information he might have been able to dig up about Leo and his friends.

"Hell of a vacation you got going there," Logan declared when he answered the phone without even a hello. But that was Logan. "Nothing like a murder to spice up a second honeymoon and your wife's birthday."

"This wouldn't have been my choice," Tanner replied, quietly closing the door between the living room and the bedroom. Maddie was in the ensuite bathroom taking a shower and the chances of her overhearing this conversation were nil, but just in case he'd close it. "I just wanted Maddie to have a good time but as usual, trouble seems to follow us. You know how that is."

Logan and Ava had had their share of trouble as well. Hopefully, it was cleared up for a long time.

"I do know how that is."

"So did you find anything?"

He could hear Logan laughing on the other end. "Hell, yes. Of course, I found stuff. I swear everyone has a past of some sort and most people couldn't take the kind of inspection that Jared and I gave your suspects."

"Then talk to me."

"So demanding. I usually get dinner first," Logan joked. "Does Maddie know what an impatient bastard you are?"

"It's one of the things she loves about me."

"I highly fucking doubt that. Now where should I start? How about with Bibi herself? She was thirty-five years old and had been married to Leo Gordon for about ten years. They had no children. Not even a dog or a cat from what we can see. Before she married Gordon, she worked for him as his administrative assistant. He was in the process of divorcing wife number two. Bibi kept herself busy volunteering at a local animal shelter and spending time with friends. She had no close family. Her parents have passed and she and a brother only spoke a few times a year from what we can see so far."

"Did she have any assets of her own?"

"Not much," Logan replied. "We're checking for a prenup but that's going to take some time. If they divorced and didn't have one, she would have come out fine. With one? Who knows? It depends on what it says."

"Tell me about Leo Gordon."

"Now this guy is interesting. He inherited money. Not a fortune, but enough that he was able to invest and also start his own business. He owns a string of dry cleaners but he handed off the day to day operations a few years ago after a mild heart attack. He lives well but not ostentatiously. He's owned that penthouse since it was built. He keeps his cars exactly three years and then trades them in. He doesn't spend crazy amounts of money and neither did Bibi. Whether that was her own idea or his, I don't know. He gives generously each year to the same animal charity where Bibi volunteered. He has no children from his previous marriages."

"No offense but that doesn't sound all that interesting to me. That sounds kind of normal."

Logan didn't take offense, laughing at Tanner's statement. "Because I haven't gotten to the interesting part yet. Give me a minute. Now Gordon has been married twice before, right? He divorced his second wife and he didn't make a fuss about the financial settlement. He handed over a chunk of money and settled the divorce case right away. No fighting."

Tanner was beginning to get that feeling in his gut. "What about his first wife?"

"Caroline Treager Gordon had been married to Leo Gordon for three years when she drowned in their swimming pool. Supposedly she was walking in her sleep and fell in the pool. Her arms and legs got tangled in her loose nightgown and she drowned."

That sounded shady.

"Sleepwalking? Do people even really do that? I thought it was something you only see in movies."

"Certain prescription pharmaceuticals can have you walking, driving, and eating in your sleep. You can even have sex in your sleep."

Who in the fuck would want to do that?

"So was Caroline Gordon under the influence of one of those drugs?"

"I don't know. I'm still working on getting more information about her death. All I have is a few newspaper reports."

"I have to say that Leo Gordon must be the unluckiest husband to have lost two young wives in his adult life. While I'm certain it could happen, the odds have to be astronomical, especially for a guy that isn't that old."

"He's sixty-two."

"That's not that old."

"I didn't say he was old, I said he was sixty-two. Damn, you're prickly. I thought a vacation was supposed to be restful."

"Not when there's a dead body. The sheriff asked me to help but I told him no."

There was a pause before Logan replied.

"Isn't that what you're doing right now?"

"I'm not helping officially," Tanner explained. "I'm just helping the guy gather some information and pointing him in the right direction. This isn't my case. I'm not a lawman anymore."

Apparently, he'd said something hilarious because Logan was howling with laughter, making Tanner pull the phone farther from his ear.

"What's so damn funny?"

"You. Saying that you're not a cop anymore. It's in your blood. Even down there on vacation, you just can't help yourself."

"Because the sheriff doesn't have any experience. If he did, I wouldn't have bothered."

"Right," Logan said, drawing out the word. "You wouldn't have cared either way. Do you even hear yourself? You miss it. But you don't have to. Come work with me and you can call your own shots. Choose your cases."

I should be jumping on this offer.

But it didn't…excite Tanner. That restlessness that he'd been feeling wasn't going to go away by taking a job with his friends. It would be different, but the same.

"I'm not ready to go back to work yet," Tanner finally said. "Give me a break. I've been working since I was fifteen. Can't I have a few weeks off before you start busting my balls?"

"You can have all the time off you want. Just name the day you want to start."

"You're *starting* to piss me off."

"I did all of this digging for you today and that's the thanks I get," Logan laughed. "I don't know how Maddie puts up with you."

"I don't know how Ava puts up with you," Tanner shot back. "She's a saint. So is Maddie, though. We married very patient women."

"We did. Now to get back to business, we're still digging into the other names you gave me. I'll have more soon."

In the meantime, there were a hell of a lot of unanswered questions.

Who was Bibi with last night?

Did her husband know? Did he care?

Did Leo Gordon kill his wife? Or did someone else do the deed?

And was Caroline Gordon's death an accident?

One thing was for certain; Gordon was looking mighty suspicious at the moment.

"Do you and Dan talk about death?"

It wasn't exactly the best way to start a conversation with her best friend but Maddie had suspicions. Strong ones. There was something about Leo's story that didn't sit well with her, and despite her husband's relaxed attitude, she couldn't shake it.

"Uh...hello to you, too. You must be having a wonderful second honeymoon if you're dwelling on death. Is Tanner being a shit or something?"

Maddie quickly filled Sherry in on what had happened. They hadn't spoken since last night.

"Holy crap," Sherry marveled. "And you think the husband did it?"

"I think that he has a highly suspicious story about his wife's wishes about death. Have you ever told Dan what kind of funeral you wanted?"

"No, but to be fair, I don't like to talk about death. At all. In fact, how can I get you to change the subject right now?"

Sherry had issues. Lots of them. Not in the least was hearing about Maddie's work where sometimes a patient didn't make it. She didn't want to think or talk about it, if at all possible.

Sighing, Maddie plopped down onto the bed, her head resting against a fluffy pillow. Tanner in the living room supposedly reading, but she could hear his muffled voice through the door. He was also talking on the phone.

"I'm sorry. I know you don't like to talk about stuff like that."

"Maddie, I don't know anyone who does," Sherry explained patiently. "I'm sure there are couples who have talked about this but Dan and I aren't one of them. We've talked about life insurance and whether I'd marry again, but not about a funeral. Frankly, he can do whatever he wants if I go first."

"That's what Tanner said. And would you marry again?"

"Maybe, but only for the sake of the children. Dan says that he couldn't marry again because I've ruined him for any other woman. What about you? Would you marry again?"

Dan was a smart man.

"I can't imagine being married to anyone else but Tanner."

"That's what I thought you'd say. So what are you going to do now? You seem really focused on this woman's death."

Maybe because it kept her mind off her own issues.

"It was just so shocking. We met her yesterday and now she's dead."

"And you want to find out who did it."

Sherry didn't phrase it as a question.

"I want Tanner to help find the killer," Maddie admitted. "The sheriff seems nice but is clueless. The murderer might get away with it. Tanner wouldn't let that happen."

The other end of the phone was quiet for a long moment and then Sherry spoke.

"I'm just going to play amateur psychiatrist here for a minute. Are you so intent on Tanner solving this murder because of this woman, or do you want him to do it because you think it will snap him back to the old Tanner before he was fired?"

"Sometimes I hate you."

"Feeling is mutual. Now answer my question. I have a feeling I struck a nerve."

Sherry had, indeed, hit a sore spot. Maddie didn't like to think that she might be right but...

"It's a possibility."

"On a scale of one to ten, with one being no possibility and ten being a whopper of a possibility where do you think you are?"

"Is the size of possibility important? Does it really matter?"

"I'll take that as a seven," Sherry said. "Maybe an eight. You do know that Tanner isn't a cop anymore, right? This murder isn't his problem or responsibility. You're supposed to be having fun. You're on vacation."

"I know, I know. But he could do it. I know he could."

"Does he not want to?"

"He seems surprisingly reluctant. He keeps saying that we're on vacation and that he'd never do that to me. As if I'm the thing holding him back. But I haven't said a word about not wanting him to do it."

"Maddie...have you thought...well...maybe he doesn't want to be a cop anymore?"

She had thought of that. Briefly. In the far recesses of her mind. She simply couldn't quite wrap her brain around it. Tanner being a sheriff was all she knew. He'd been the sheriff for as long as she could remember.

"That's a possibility, too."

"On a scale of one to ten, with one—"

"Stop," Maddie begged. "Let's just be okay with it's a possibility."

"Fine. So you're not going to the wake tonight?"

Even two thousand miles away and on the phone, Maddie could hear disapproval in Sherry's tone.

"You think I should go," Maddie sighed. "You think I'm being impolite."

"No," Sherry snorted. "You barely know these people and you'll never see them again. Go or don't go. It's fine. I'm just thinking that if you go you might find out a bit more about this Gordon guy. It might help you figure out if he's a killer or not."

"I'm not the detective."

"Why not? Ava helps Logan all the time. Maybe if you showed some enthusiasm for solving the case, Tanner might feel more free to do the same."

Sherry had a point. It wasn't the worst idea in the world.

They could stop in to the wake tonight and have a look around. Talk to a few people. Hear what they were saying. If what Ashley had told her was true, Gordon's own friends might suspect him.

"I'll do it."

CHAPTER TWELVE

Tanner hadn't said much when Maddie had told him that she thought they ought to go to the wake for Bibi. He hadn't seemed surprised or dismayed or glad or…anything. He'd simply nodded and said that it was probably the polite thing to do. He was certainly keeping his emotions under wraps these days. He'd never been a man with super-highs and lower-than-lows but it was as if he was training to become a poker player.

She could hear him in the bedroom getting dressed while she put on her makeup in the bathroom. They'd brought a set of dressy clothes since they were planning to go out to a fancy dinner on her birthday, which made getting ready rather easy. She had the one dress and a pair of matching shoes. That was it. She had no decisions to make except what shade of lipstick – of the two she'd brought – to wear. A bright red or a subdued nude? She was leaning toward the nude since this was a more somber event than a birthday dinner.

Stroking mascara over her lashes, she let her mind drift to tonight and what she would say to Leo Gordon. How to express her condolences to a man that might have killed his wife? It wasn't as straightforward as she would have wished it to be.

Tanner stuck his head into the bathroom. "Are you almost ready to go?"

"Just lipstick and my shoes, then I'll be ready. Do you need help with your tie?"

"I got it." He stepped into the bathroom, his gaze running from her toes to the top of her head. This time he wasn't hiding that he liked what he saw. "Damn, you're a beautiful woman."

She waved her mascara wand at him. "Don't you start. We have to go to this party. We don't have time for whatever it is you're planning."

"We'll have time afterward. We don't have to stay very long."

"It's a date." She hesitated for a moment but then decided to plunge right in. She wasn't fond of his closed-mouthed mood of late. "Are you mad that I said we should go?"

Pinching his brows together, Tanner shook his head. "Of course not. Why would you think that I'm mad?"

Sighing, Maddie shrugged her shoulders. She didn't really want to get into it with him right now but she'd been avoiding this conversation for so long it was beginning to feel like years, even though she knew it hadn't been more than six months or so. She'd been waiting for him to snap out of whatever it was that was getting him up before dawn every single day.

This isn't the time or place.

But I'm tired of waiting.

Too bad. Don't start something that you can't finish.

"It's not important. Give me a minute and then we'll go."

Frankly, she and Tanner rarely argued. One of them usually compromised and it all worked out. But this wasn't a restaurant that one of them didn't want to eat at. This felt like more.

Turning on his heel, Tanner moved toward the door but before she could even reach for her lipstick tube the words tumbled out of her mouth before she could stop them.

"I know that you get up before dawn every morning."

He stopped, his back to her, tension in his shoulders. She didn't say anything else, simply waiting for him to respond. After a few beats, he turned around, his expression almost panicked.

"Why didn't you say something?"

Was he kidding?

"I'll ask you the same question, Tanner. Why didn't you say something? I waited for you to tell me that you were having bouts of insomnia but you never did. The only thing I could conclude from that was that you were getting up for a specific reason. Maybe you didn't want to have morning sex, or maybe I snored too much. I didn't have any clue why you were doing it but it was clear to me that you didn't want me to know about it. And that's what bothered me. My husband keeping secrets. That isn't the man that I know. Or thought I did, anyway."

By the time she was finished she was breathing fast, her anger and frustration building with every word and sentence. She'd been keeping this all inside for far too long and the dam was breaking.

"And it's not just you getting up early and not telling me about it. It's more than that. You've been acting strangely for months. Then you get fired and you almost rip our house apart with improvement projects. I was afraid to come home at night because I didn't know what I was going to find. When you suggested this vacation, I jumped on it because that meant that you couldn't rip up the baseboards while we were in Florida."

His lips quirked up in an almost smile. "You're angry with me."

"I'm frustrated with you."

"You're angry, too. It's okay to admit it."

In a few steps she was right in front of him, poking his chest with her finger.

"I don't need your permission to be angry, Tanner Marks. I'm a grown woman and I can be as furious as I want to be, thank you very much."

"I've always known that, Maddie."

Tears were burning her eyes. She always cried when she was mad and she hated that. Now he was going to think she was sad when she was simply angry with him.

"Did you? Because every time I've been mad at you, you either back down or you give me some lecture about how you're older and I should trust your wisdom. Just so we're clear...your wisdom sometimes lets you down."

"Damn, I've fucked this up." He rubbed the back of his neck and then reached for her hand, leading her into the bedroom. Tugging her down on the mattress, they sat side by side. "I think we need to start at the beginning."

"I don't even know where the beginning is."

She sniffled and he reached across her to the tissue box on the bedside table, snatching one from the box to hand to her.

"I messed up my first marriage, Maddie. A lot of our problems were my fault. My drinking. My job. The pressures of being a military wife and then a cop's wife. I could have done a hell of a lot better and when you and I got married I swore that I'd do better this time. I'd do everything right." Chuckling, Tanner shook his head. "That I'd be the perfect husband because I knew deep down that you could do so much better than me."

She'd heard him say some of this before. That he hadn't been the best husband and father but that he hadn't been the worst, either. He wished he'd been more in tune with how his decisions affected his family.

"There's no such thing as the perfect husband. I'm certainly not the perfect wife, and I've never once thought to myself that I could do any better than you. I love you, Tanner."

The anger and frustration were draining away as quickly as it had risen up, but that was always the way. She couldn't stay mad at this man even when she should.

"And I love you, Madison Shay. I wanted to be such a good husband. I never wanted you to regret marrying me."

"I don't regret marrying you, but I'm not sure what this has to do with you acting strangely these past months." A terrible thought occurred to her, her heart clutching in her chest. "Do you regret marrying me?"

He grabbed her hand and lifted it to his warm lips. "Never. Not for a single solitary second. I was just trying to frame what I had to say. I wanted to be such a great husband for you and I'm not sure that I really have been. Sometimes…I feel like I've let you down, Maddie."

Where on earth did he get that idea?

"Did I make you feel that way?"

She was already yelling at herself when he firmly shook his head. "No, you haven't done anything. It's just a feeling. When I got fired, all I could hear in my head was my old man saying that a real man provides for his family. Yet, I wasn't providing for you. I wasn't taking care of you and Amanda. You were taking care of us, and if I'm honest, the reason we're so financially comfortable is because of you. With the house mortgage-free and your medical practice, my salary as a sheriff was merely an afterthought."

"You've worked hard all your life—"

"I know," he broke in. "Everyone says that I deserve some time off but it doesn't feel that way. That's why I was doing all that stuff around the house. I wanted to feel like I was contributing, that I was taking care of my family."

A few tears slipped down her cheeks. "You take care of us

just fine."

Leaning forward, he rested his elbows on his knees. "Baby, I am so fucked up. I feel…shit…I don't even know if I can describe it. I feel…restless. I can't tell you why but that's how I feel. It's like an itch I can't scratch or reach. It's been driving me crazy and I didn't want to tell you. That's why I've been getting up before dawn, Maddie. I can't sleep because I'm thinking about my life and trying to figure out what in the hell my problem is. I didn't want to tell you about it because I'm embarrassed as fuck that I might be having a mid-life crisis. That's what Sam said. He said that I was having a midlife crisis and I told him that was bullshit. My dad didn't have a midlife crisis and I don't think my grandpa did, either. It's crazy to even think it. I have nothing to have a crisis about. I have a great life with a wonderful wife and kids but there's that restlessness that I can't pin down and I sure as shit can't get rid of. No matter how hard I try."

It was the most he'd spoken at one time in months. Maybe years. Her husband wasn't one to go on and on about his *feelings*. That wasn't his way but clearly some emotions had been building inside of him, too. They were quite a pair.

What was crazier than going through a midlife crisis herself?

Tanner Marks having one.

This…she hadn't expected. But boy, did it explain a whole hell of a lot.

It looked like they both needed to talk.

Preferably to each other.

CHAPTER THIRTEEN

T anner had finally spoken the words out loud. He'd told his wife that he might be having a midlife crisis.

And it made him sound like a huge emotionally needy wuss.

If Maddie was thinking about how to divorce his ass, he wouldn't be surprised.

He'd made her cry, too. He hated when that happened and he usually did everything in his power to make sure he didn't do it. She was right, though. He always tried to make sure they didn't fight. Even if it meant burying any issues they might have. It looked like it had all caught up with them, though.

"Do you want to hear something funny?" Maddie said, her hand gliding up and down his back in a soothing motion. He wasn't feeling relaxed, though. If he could jump out of his skin, he'd do it right now. "I've been feeling sort of restless myself. I just want to slow life down and make it last. I want to savor it but it just keeps flying by. I told Sherry about it and she told me that I was probably going through a midlife crisis. It looks like we're doing it together. It's kind of romantic in a weird and twisted way."

His sweet Maddie. She could make him laugh at the strangest

of times.

"She told you that you were going through a midlife crisis? You're not old enough. You're only–"

"Forty," Maddie interrupted, moving her hand abruptly from where she'd been massaging his shoulders. "Forty years old, Tanner. As in not a child or a teenager or even a young woman. I'm a middle-aged wife and mother. Forty is middle-aged. I am not the same age as when you married me, but I swear, you will always think that you are wiser than I am. I'll be eighty and you'll be ninety-five and you'll still pull the wisdom card on me."

Ouch. Was he that bad? No…maybe. He ran through dozens of their conversations in his recent memory and he didn't like what he saw.

"I've been dismissive," Tanner said with a groan. "I haven't been listening, have I?"

"No, you haven't."

"I'm listening now."

"I thought we were talking about you."

"My problems can wait."

"So can mine." She turned toward him, their knees pressed together. "We've already started you so let's get that done first. You said that you're feeling restless but you don't know why."

He didn't know why but damn, he'd given it a hell of a lot of thought these past weeks.

"I'm glad I got fired."

The words were blunt and to the point. He'd never admitted them to himself but with Maddie he felt safe enough to say them out loud.

It was true. He was glad.

Whatever Maddie had been expecting him to say, that wasn't it. Her eyes were wide with shock and her mouth had fallen open.

"I'm glad I got fired," he repeated. That repressive weight that he'd been carrying around on his shoulders for months was suddenly lifted away. He felt better already. "It's hard for me to admit but it's the truth."

"You don't like being a sheriff anymore?"

"I don't know how to explain it." He jumped to his feet and began to pace the narrow area between the bed and the door. "I'm so mixed up about it all. I've done what I'm supposed to do. I followed the rules, Maddie. I went to work every day and gave it my all, and I did it for years. That's what you're supposed to do, right? But in the end, I didn't feel...shit...I don't know what I'm supposed to feel. All I know is this feeling started when I came home after the manhunt for Bryson."

He didn't expect her to understand and it was easy to see that she was struggling with what he was saying, her brows furrowed.

"Are you saying that you don't feel appreciated for all that you've done?"

"Fuck no," he said with a shake of his head. "If anything, I've been too appreciated. All the articles in the newspapers and magazines. I feel like I can't go anywhere without people recognizing my name. I hate that shit. No, it's something else and I wish I could put my finger on it. It's the feeling that...there's more."

"A new challenge?"

"Maybe. I'm not sure. I'm just not as content to live my life the way I have been. I feel like I've been following everyone else's rules all my life. I want to make a few rules of my own, but I'm not even sure what that would look like or what I would do. Let's face it. The only thing I'm trained for is law enforcement work. That's it. Logan's begging me to come work with them and I should want to do it..."

"But you don't," Maddie finished for him. "You didn't tell me that. I've been wondering if they called and offered you a job."

"They did but something is holding me back from taking it."

"If you're not excited to do it, then you're right to hesitate. I don't want you taking a job for the sake of having a job. I love what I do and I want you to feel the same." She tilted her head, her gaze steady on him. "If you hadn't been fired, what were you going to do?"

"Lie to myself," Tanner replied promptly. "I was planning to continue doing what I'm supposed to do until I retired. End of story."

"Tanner," she sighed. "That's terrible."

"It's no worse than a lot of people. Most don't go to jobs they love, Maddie-mine. They go because they need a paycheck."

"You don't need to do that."

"I need my pride."

"Society and your father have a lot to answer for. You've been brainwashed to think your only value is in bringing home the bacon."

"Probably."

She pointed to his cell phone that was sitting on the bedside table. "If you're getting the same messages that I am, you have to know that when we get back the new mayor – whoever that is – is going to offer you your old job back."

"I know."

"I don't want you to take it if you don't want it."

She made it sound so easy. Don't do what you don't want to.

"I don't know anything else."

"I don't believe that. You have many marketable skills." She began counting on her fingers. "Leadership, organization, people management, analysis. That's just a few. I bet I could think of a lot more if we took our time."

"And all of those skills add up to the job of sheriff. I think my going back is inevitable."

Maddie stood, throwing up her hands. "So that's your plan? You're going to go back to Springwood, go back to a job that you hate, feel restless, and get up at five in the morning every day until you die? That's the plan?"

Well…shit.

"When you say it like that it sounds stupid. When I said it in my head, it sounded so much smarter."

"It's not," she snorted. "You know what they say the definition of insanity is?"

"Doing the same thing over and over and expecting a different result," he sighed. "So now I'm insane, too. That's just fantastic."

"So don't take your old job back."

"And do what? Because I have to do something. I've been ripping the house apart because I want to feel fucking productive. I'm going to need something to do every day."

She stood in front of him, her smile slowly widening on her face. "Then run for mayor."

What? Wait…no. No, he couldn't do that. Could he?

"Mayor? I don't know shit about being mayor."

"Yes, you do. You certainly know more than Pete did when he was elected. You've lived in Springwood your entire life and you know the ins and outs better than almost anyone. You said you wanted to make some of your own rules. This is your chance. You can help your neighbors and at the same time find that something more that you've been seeking."

Mayor. It wasn't the worst idea he'd ever heard but…

"Who would vote for me? I mean…besides you."

Throwing her head back, Maddie laughed until tears ran out

of her eyes. "Are you kidding? Everyone would vote for you. It would be a landslide victory. You're revered in our little town, Tanner. You'd win if you ran. The job would be just up your alley. Leadership, organization, people management. It was practically made for you. You could really make a difference but in a different way."

It would be different. No less important. He might even be able to make improvements to the town that would last long after he was gone.

The first thing he'd do is hire Sam as the sheriff.

"You're thinking about it, aren't you? You're thinking that you want to do it."

"I am," he admitted. "I would never had considered it until you mentioned it but you have a point. I could make a real difference in Springwood."

"And it would be a new challenge."

"It certainly would be."

"But?"

"Why don't I want to be a sheriff anymore?"

It was an inelegant question but it summed up his feelings. Luckily, his wife didn't laugh at him, instead taking his query as seriously as he'd meant it.

"Maybe...maybe because you've already done it. Think about it this way. Perhaps the reason that you're restless after the manhunt for Wade Bryson is that was pretty much the pinnacle of police work. Bringing in a serial killer that was on the run. It doesn't get much more dangerous and exciting than that. I would imagine everything else sort of pales in comparison. You've been a wonderful sheriff, but you've done that. It's okay to want something different. It's okay to say that you're ready to do a new thing. Maybe that's what a midlife crisis is. Saying goodbye to the comfortable, safe, and known and taking on that next stage of life."

His wife's eyes had filled with tears and she sat down heavily onto the mattress, burying her face in her hands.

"Honey, are you okay?"

It was a stupid question because he could easily see that she wasn't. For some reason her impassioned speech had made her sad and he didn't have a clue as to why.

She looked up, her cheeks wet. "No, I am not okay. I just realized something."

"That your husband's an idiot?"

Rolling her eyes, she gave him a long-suffering sigh. "I realized that my midlife crisis is about being scared to go to that next scary stage in life."

Good. Now they were going to talk about her instead of him. All this introspection was annoying.

Sitting down next to her, he reached for her hands, wrapping their cold flesh in his own.

"What are you afraid of, babe?"

Sniffling, she leaned her head against his arm. "Of Amanda growing up. Of me getting old. Of not being a good enough mother or wife or doctor or friend. I'm scared of falling asleep one day and waking up and Amanda is leaving for college and I missed it all. Everything."

Whoa. That was a boatload of fears.

"You're a wonderful wife and mother. You're a terrific doctor and I know that Sherry thinks you're a great friend. Where is all of this coming from?"

"Amanda started kindergarten. She's not a baby anymore." A fresh spate of tears began and he reached for another tissue. "And I know what you're going to say. You're going to tell me that kids are supposed to grow up but frankly, I don't want to hear that. It's all going so fast and I can't slow it down. I just want to slow it down a little bit."

Had he become so preachy and predictable that he would have dismissed his own wife's fears? It looked like he had and he wasn't happy about that. She'd said that he would always use the wisdom card. He needed to stop that right now. As in yesterday.

"It goes quick, doesn't it?" he mused, wrapping an arm around Maddie and pulling her closer. The familiar scent of her strawberry shampoo tickled his nostrils. "One day you're thirty and I'm forty-five and the next we're ten years older and our daughter is starting kindergarten. I wish it could slow down, too. I wish we could work less and savor more of our lives, especially when Amanda is so young. It doesn't seem fair that when we get older and the kids are out of the house that's when we have more free time."

She dashed at her wet cheeks with the back of her hand. "It isn't fair. I want more time with her now. She's growing up so fast and I'm afraid we're going to look up and miss it all."

He opened his mouth to tell Maddie that there would be plenty more milestones to make her feel this way – middle school, proms, graduation – just to name a few, but he shut it just as quickly.

The wisdom card. He wasn't going to play it again. He didn't have to be right or offer advice every single time she talked about her troubles. She wasn't asking him to solve her problems, she was asking him to listen.

Besides, no one could actually slow down time, but they could make a few adjustments so that they weren't looking at their life in the rearview mirror all of the time.

"Then let's make more time," he said. "Let's do that. Let's arrange our life so that we have more time with Amanda."

"How? How would be even do that?"

"You could work less. We'd be okay. We could tighten our

belts a little. Then you'd have more time with her. I have to admit that one of the bright spots of being fired was that I got to spend more time with our daughter. That's been a lot of fun. I missed so much with Emily and Chris."

His wife was frowning but not because she was unhappy. She was thinking about how to make it work. He could practically hear the wheels in her head turning over idea after idea.

"I suppose I could work only when Amanda is in school, but I don't think I could get away with it five days a week. Maybe three." She pulled up her legs, sitting crisscross on the mattress. "What I really need to do is attract another doctor to the practice."

Tanner had said that same thing about a year and a half ago but he wasn't about to remind her of that now.

"You've been working some crazy hours," he agreed. "You don't have to kill yourself for the good residents of Springwood. They don't expect that."

And if they did, they had their priorities screwed up.

"I just want to make sure that they're taken care of."

"You're not the only doctor in town. You're the best doctor but not the only one. They'll be taken care of."

She nudged his shoulder. "You have to say that. You're my husband."

"I don't have to but yes, I am your husband. Your proud husband. You make me very happy, Madison."

Lifting her up, he settled her on his lap. They didn't get near enough time alone with one another.

"You make me happy, too."

"Even when I'm ripping the house apart?"

"Even then." She took a deep breath and let it out slowly. "That's a lot of sharing we've just done there. It was exhausting."

"We don't have to go tonight. We can stay right here."

She shook her head. "I think we should go…and I think you should help the sheriff. Because he badly needs it. It's almost like fate that you're staying here, don't you think?"

It wouldn't hurt to help Ken Smith. Now that Tanner had admitted – out loud – that he didn't really want to be a cop anymore it made helping the young sheriff much easier. Maddie wouldn't expect him to go back to Springwood and take his old job back.

"I think you're right. I can help him a little bit."

"Didn't he leave you a business card? You should call him. You can start helping him tonight when we're at the wake."

"Celebration of life," he corrected. "But that's a good idea. I'll call him and then we'll go. Are you ready?"

For the first time in a long while, Tanner was ready to face the future.

With Maddie by his side.

CHAPTER FOURTEEN

Leo's penthouse condo was wall to wall bodies when Maddie and Tanner arrived at Bibi's celebration of life. The double doors to the patio were open and every now and then a fresh breeze would waft through the open floor plan, washing away the cloying mixture of perfume and scented candles that hung in the air.

And there were lots of candles. All over the house, but mostly at the far end of the living room where Leo had built something of a shrine to his recently late wife. There were several photos of her blown up to poster size and placed on stands, plus a small table of Bibi's "Favorites" – books she loved, jewelry she liked. There was even a tablet computer set up to show a looped slideshow of photos from Leo and Bibi's travels.

"It's so sad," Ashley said, sidling up next to Maddie. "I helped Leo put this together and I swear I've cried all day long."

"It is sad," Maddie agreed. If Ashley had been crying all day, she sure knew how to hide it. She ought to give makeup tips because her face and eye makeup was flawless. "It was so sweet of you to help Leo."

Ashley shrugged, taking a sip of her drink, something fruity with orange juice. "The two of them were such good friends to me when I moved into the building. I just wanted to give a little something back."

"It's a lovely party. You've done an amazing job in such a short amount of time."

"I called in a few favors."

The small talk was awkward. Maddie wasn't the best at it, preferring real conversations to shallow ones.

"I saw you and your husband talking to the sheriff this morning."

Looked like they were going to have a real discussion now. The polite chatter was done.

"Yes, we did speak with him."

"You talked to him a long time. I mean…for someone that didn't know Bibi and had really only met her once."

Was Ashley probing for information? Interesting.

"The sheriff recognized Tanner's name."

Frowning, Ashley looked confused. "Recognized his name? Is he some sort of celebrity? I didn't realize."

Normally Maddie didn't like talking about Tanner's exploits as a sheriff but at this moment she didn't mind.

"He was one of the men that brought in the serial killer Wade Bryson. It was in a lot of the papers and magazines."

Her eyes wide, Ashley almost choked on her drink, sputtering and coughing. "Wade Bryson? I had no idea. That's…wow. You must be so proud."

"I am. Tanner is a great lawman."

Ashley didn't appear to know what to say next. She opened her mouth and then shut it a few times before finally getting some words out.

"So he and the sheriff must have had a lot to talk about."

"He asked Tanner to consult on this case."

They had discussed this before arriving at the party and after talking to the sheriff. Tanner was officially helping out and there was no reason to keep it a secret. They'd all be finding out pretty quickly because he was planning on starting to ask questions tonight.

"He did?" Ashley's brows were almost at her hairline. "Well…that's fantastic. The case will be wrapped up that much faster. Maybe even before Leo leaves."

Leaves? Leo was going somewhere?

"Leo is leaving?"

"He's going to visit some friends in New York City. Help get his mind off of this tragedy. I can't imagine having to live in a house all by myself where I'd lived with my deceased spouse. That would be awful. I think he's made the right call. Getting out of here and seeing some old friends is just what he needs to help him move on."

Maddie couldn't imagine a scenario where she would leave if the police were investigating Tanner's murder.

If you ask me? That's shady behavior.

"When does he plan to go?"

"Wednesday if he can get everything sewn up by then. I'll help him all that I can."

That didn't leave Tanner much time to investigate the new widower.

Was that Leo's plan?

Tanner couldn't get anywhere near Leo for almost half an hour after arriving to the party. The man was constantly surrounded by friends giving their condolences so he hung back until the right time. This was going to be tricky, expressing his own sympathy and also informing Leo that he was joining the investigation. It wouldn't be ethical not to tell him.

"I'm so sorry for your loss," Tanner said when Leo was finally alone. "I can't imagine what you're going through right now. I know how I'd feel if I ever lost Maddie."

Nodding sadly, Leo leaned against the back of the leather sofa. "Thank you. Bibi was really special. A wonderful woman. She's going to be missed a great deal, not just by me but by her friends."

Tanner let his gaze wander the room, filled with people. "It certainly seems that she was loved. It's good to have your friends around as well during this difficult time."

"They've been a godsend. I wouldn't have been able to pull this together if it weren't for Ashley. She's a force of nature."

"It's good to have friends like that."

Leo nodded again. "I've been so busy making phone calls to friends and family to let them know about Bibi I haven't had much time to process what's happened. That's probably a good thing. I keep waiting for her to walk in the front door and tell me about her day."

"The sooner the police bring in the person who did this the better you'll be able to find closure. At least, that's my experience."

"You were a cop, I believe you said? I'll take your word for it. Right now, that seems very unimportant. Arresting the man that did this isn't going to bring Bibi back."

Tanner had been a police officer for a damn long time. In all of those years he'd rarely had anyone tell him that they didn't care if the person that had murdered a loved one was caught or not. There had been a few, of course, but he hadn't found it the norm. It didn't help that already Leo was a suspect, purely statistically speaking. The spouse was always the first one to be investigated.

"It won't but Bibi deserves justice." Shifting on his feet, Tanner steeled himself for Leo's reaction to his next statement. "I feel so strongly about that I agreed to help Sheriff Ken Smith with this murder investigation. I have a great deal of experience with this sort of thing and after meeting Bibi I feel that I can contribute in a positive way."

Leo clutched at his heart, his eyes widening in surprise. "Jesus, that's… I don't even know what to say. You only met Bibi yesterday and you're willing to do this. That's…fucking fantastic. Ken Smith is a good man but he's inexperienced, a new sheriff. He can use all the help he can get."

It appeared that Leo was actually tearing up at Tanner's declaration. Whether the gratitude was genuine or a put-on, it would look to anyone watching to be sincere and heartfelt.

"I'll do the best I can while I'm here," Tanner replied. "Hopefully I can point Sheriff Smith in the right direction. In fact, to that end, I'd like to speak with you. I have a few questions that would help me tremendously."

"Of course, of course." Leo looked around the room and then pointed to the hallway. "Let's go somewhere more private. My office is just down there. It will be a hell of a lot more quiet."

Tanner followed Leo down a long hallway and into a small office with a view of the water. Most of the room was taken up with the large dark oak desk and the bookshelves behind it, but the far wall was basically one giant window. Leo motioned for Tanner to have a seat while he took the chair behind the desk.

Ah, the old power play. I know it well. Sorry, but I'm not intimidated so easily.

"So what kind of questions did you need to ask me?" Leo said, leaning back in the large leather chair. He'd spoken up before Tanner even had a chance to.

Another power move. Trying to take control of the conversation from the outset. Wanting to be the alpha male – large and in charge. Sometimes, it was useful to let your suspect think they were in control. That might be a useful tactic here.

We'll see.

"When was the last time you saw your wife alive?"

"When I went to bed," Leo answered promptly. "I retired earlier than Bibi which wasn't unusual. She was a night owl and I'm an early bird. We've been keeping that schedule for years and last night was no different. I went to bed and she stayed up reading or watching television."

That was one long-winded answer to a simple question. Perhaps he'd already answered the same to Ken Smith.

"Did you hear her come to bed?"

"I'm a heavy sleeper. I didn't hear anything but once again, that's not unusual."

"So for all you know Bibi never came to bed?"

"That's very possible."

Leo looked far too comfortable answering these questions. Confident and at ease.

"I want to make sure that I have the timeline correct. Bibi was home when you went to bed, correct?"

"Yes, of course she was."

Shit. Because Tanner didn't know just what Bibi was doing last night this was a particularly delicate subject. She might have simply been with a friend and it was all innocent. Or not. And if it wasn't, just how much did Leo know? Had the sheriff mentioned to him that Bibi had been seen walking down the beach?

"Did Bibi ever go out after you'd gone to bed? Maybe to have a drink with some friends or see a late movie, perhaps?"

"No, she would never do that. Bibi didn't like to drive at

night."

"What about walking down the beach to see a neighbor? To the pub on the corner?"

"No, I don't think so, especially after dark."

This was the part in any sort of investigation that Tanner hated. It didn't have to be a murder. It could be a robbery or even something as small as a kid shoplifting a candy bar from the corner store. But somehow, he got stuck telling one family member that another family member was doing something that they didn't know about.

Whether by design or accident. It didn't matter which, it only mattered that Tanner had to be the bad guy today. He might as well just man up and do it. It appeared that the sheriff hadn't said a word to Leo.

"It's just that when Maddie and I were walking along the beach last night we saw Bibi and another person going into another building not far away."

Leo's puzzled expression disappeared and he smiled. "I see what you're getting at here. The sheriff did mention that someone had supposedly seen Bibi on the beach last night but I didn't pay much attention to that. I know that she was home. It was dark and you must have mistaken her for someone else."

Tanner had many flaws – far too many to catalog to Leo – but the one thing he'd been blessed with was fantastic distance vision. Now over fifty, he needed reading glasses but his distance vision was still as sharp as when he was a teenager.

He'd seen Bibi last night. There was no mistake. Maddie had seen her as well. Arguing with Leo, however, wouldn't get them anywhere. Either Leo truly didn't know that Bibi was out and about last night or he was in some state of denial. It was interesting that Leo didn't grab onto this news, though. It would have given him plausible deniability that he was responsible for his wife's death.

"It was dark," Tanner finally said. "I suppose I could have been mistaken."

But I'm not.

"Can you tell me if Bibi was acting differently in the last few weeks? Maybe she changed up her routine or complained about someone at the local coffee shop or gym? Did she recently argue with anyone? Even a minor disagreement?"

Shifting in his chair, Leo's gaze fell to the floor. "I hate to even say it because I know it was an innocent thing."

"I'm sure it is and the sooner we rule it out, the better off we'll be."

He looked up, rubbing the back of his neck. "That night at the party after you and your wife left, Bibi and Ashley got into it a little bit. It wasn't a big deal but there were raised voices. Ashley left shortly after but I know she wouldn't do something like this. There's no way."

Although Tanner hadn't seen the coroner's report, he was inclined to agree. Strangling another person to death was far more physical than most people realized. Ashley appeared to be in excellent shape but unless Bibi was incapacitated in some way, he couldn't see her being able to overcome the struggle and get it done without anyone hearing or seeing.

"Do you know what they argued about?"

"I didn't hear all of it. I was out on the patio. It was something about Ashley getting married again."

"Is she getting married again?"

"Not that I know of. I just think Bibi was pushing Ashley to get married again but for love this time. Ashley's all about finding a rich man and she doesn't try to hide that. She's quite out in the open about her ambitions."

Maddie had mentioned it. As far as Tanner was concerned if

the woman wanted to marry money that was her business.

But she'd probably earn it. One way or another.

"Anything else?" Tanner prompted. "Even the littlest item might be the break we need. Have you had anything delivered lately?"

Frowning, Leo nodded. "We bought a new dining room table about a week ago. We gave the old one to a charity organization. I'd never liked it and Bibi agreed that we would replace it."

"And they delivered it?"

"Yes, why do you ask?"

"Perhaps one of them came back. It's happened before, although usually it's more about robbery than murder."

"Is that what you think this is? A robbery gone wrong? They did take Bibi's wedding ring and her diamond tennis bracelet."

No, that wasn't what Tanner thought it was. Bibi had been found outside the penthouse and it didn't appear that there had been any break-in. The killer could have taken the jewelry to make it look like a robbery or as a memento.

"I have to check every angle. I want to be thorough while I'm here."

"I'm so grateful that you're helping. Ken Smith is a good guy but I don't think he's ever handled a murder before. This is a small town and it's usually quiet."

"I'll do the best that I can. I just have a few more questions if you don't mind."

"Not at all but I hope we're almost done. I have guests out there."

"Just a couple more."

"Fine, go ahead."

This part never got any easier, but it had to be done.

"How did you and your wife get along? Were you having any

marital problems?"

The other man's face turned red and his hands tightened into fists. Tanner had definitely hit a nerve and pissed Leo off. He didn't like this part of the job but he'd be remiss in not doing it.

"The reason I ask," Tanner went on, "is that statistically speaking, the spouse is always the first suspect. The sooner we can rule you out, the better. So if you can help me with that, I can move on and investigate other leads."

"I did not kill my wife," Leo said through gritted teeth. "I loved my wife. As for being cleared, I didn't realize that I was a suspect. I was asleep when this all happened."

"Can anyone corroborate that?"

"No, do you have anyone that saw me outside last night?"

"No," Tanner admitted. "Not that I know of."

"Then it looks like I don't have to prove anything." Leo stood, his arms crossed over his chest. "I think this interview is over. If you want to talk to me, you can contact my attorney from now on."

Lawyering up. Probably a smart move on Leo's part.

"I'm sorry about the indelicate questions. It's part of the job."

"Then you have a lousy job," Leo shot back. "I just lost my wife and you're asking if we had any issues. All marriages have issues."

"That's true, but not all wives end up dead." Tanner stood as well, stepping toward the door to the office. "This must be especially terrible for you, losing another wife so young."

Leo's eyes widened and Tanner heard his swift intake of breath.

"I have no idea what you're talking about."

Really? He wanted to play it like that. Okay.

"I'll let you know if I have any more questions. There are

several people that I still need to speak to."

"Are you going to be bothering our friends?" Leo demanded, his lips a flat line. "I don't want you harassing them."

All the friendliness had disappeared from Leo's demeanor. The battle lines were clearly drawn.

"A murder investigation isn't classified as harassment, and yes, I'm going to be talking to them."

If they're going to tell me something you don't want me to know, now is the time to say it.

"I think it's time you leave my home."

Tanner had been waiting for the invitation to go fuck himself and here it was.

"I'll collect my wife and do that. I am sorry for your loss."

It's time for me to go, but I'll be back.

Time to ask the friends some questions. Leo said his marriage was fine. Tanner had a feeling that a few others might have a far different opinion.

CHAPTER FIFTEEN

Tanner had hustled Maddie out of the wake-slash-celebration of life and down the street to the small cafe on the corner near the bank. The menu wasn't huge but the smells coming out of the kitchen were downright delicious. Maddie settled on a grilled chicken sandwich with house fries and Tanner had the smoked brisket platter.

"Where did you disappear to?" Maddie asked him once they'd put their orders in. "I couldn't find you and then suddenly you were rushing us out of the door."

"Let's just say that I don't think we'll be invited over anymore. Leo wasn't happy with me and asked me to vacate the premises."

"You asked some tough questions."

"Yes, and I didn't like myself when I was doing it but they couldn't go on unasked. I have a feeling that Ken didn't ask those questions."

"*Those questions?* About the state of their marriage?"

"Bingo. We were doing fine up until then, but when I asked that he got real pissy real fast. Not a happy camper."

"What did he say about us seeing Bibi last night?"

Tanner grinned and took a drink of his iced tea. "He said that we were obviously mistaken."

"Mistaken?"

"Mistaken," Tanner confirmed. "As in *you can't believe your lying eyes*. He said that it was dark and it must have been someone else."

"What do you think? Do you think that we're wrong?"

"No. Do you think that you're wrong? Are you second-guessing it?"

Thinking back to the scene last night, Maddie shook her head. "It was Bibi. I saw her clearly. Unless she has a twin. That's the one case you've never had, Tanner. An evil twin."

"It was only a matter of time before I got one. I can't tell if Leo is in denial about Bibi being out last night or if he's just play-acting."

"Do you think he's innocent?"

"Too early to tell. I think his behavior is suspect but we don't put people in jail for acting strangely. If so, we'd have a full house and then some."

"I don't know if I should tell you this," Maddie said, wincing at her news. "If you hadn't ran us out of there, I would have told you back at the condo."

"Told me what?"

"According to Ashley, Leo is leaving on Wednesday. Going to New York City to visit friends for awhile. So…no hurry solving the case or anything."

"Shit," Tanner sighed.

"Yep, shit. You probably have more questions for Leo now."

"The first one would be to ask what's his hurry." Tanner nudged her leg with his foot. "Good job on getting that information, though. You might make a decent detective if you weren't such an amazing doctor."

Maddie sniffed disdainfully. "Ava isn't the only one that can help. I can help, too."

"Careful or I'll take you up on it."

Really?

"I wouldn't mind. For real. We could…work together. It might be fun."

Tanner's brows rose. "Or it could be dangerous. There's a killer running around loose, remember? I don't mind you giving me tidbits of information but you're not going to put yourself into harm's way."

"That goes for you, too." Maddie wagged a finger at her husband. "We're supposed to be on vacation, so no getting hurt or killed. Promise?"

"Promise. Should we pinky-swear or something? That's what I did when I was a kid."

"I'll take your word for it. Did you find out anything when you talked to Leo or was it a waste of time?"

"Funny how you mentioned Ashley. Leo said that after you and I left last night Bibi and Ashley got into an argument. He said he's not sure what about though, but there were raised voices. He assured me that Ashley wasn't a killer."

"I didn't get the killer vibe from her either, not that I would know what it was if I did. She didn't act strangely today or anything."

Their meals were slid in front of them, the aroma making Maddie's stomach growl. It had been hours since she'd last eaten.

"How would we know if they were acting strangely?" Tanner asked. "We just met these people."

"True." Maddie took a bite of her chicken sandwich and groaned. "This is so good. I'm starving."

"Save room for dessert. I saw chocolate cake on the menu. We can share it."

"Maybe I want my own piece."

Laughing, Tanner bit into a fry. "Then honey, you can have your very own. I was just thinking it might be nice to share."

He gave her a lascivious wink that had her giggling. He could be so goofy at times and she loved it.

"So what do you do now? What are the next steps?"

"First I need to talk to Ken Smith. Find out what questions he's already asked and I also need to get a copy of the coroner's report the minute it comes in. Then we need to talk to Leo and Bibi's friends. In the meantime, Jason and Logan are digging for more background information, including finances. Remember why people get murdered?"

"Love, sex, revenge, or money. Did I get it right?"

"You certainly did. You've been listening and learning. I would add power to that list, too. It's sort of like money but it has a nuance all its own. Of course, there's always the chance that this was simply a crime of opportunity. It doesn't happen often but it does happen."

Had Bibi been in the wrong place at the wrong time? Or had someone planned her murder? Hopefully, Tanner could find out.

Quickly.

Ken Smith had a copy of the preliminary coroner's report messengered over first thing in the morning so Tanner was able to read it over coffee. He and Maddie sat outside at the exact same table where they'd seen Bibi's body the morning before. It was hard to believe that this was only the third day of their vacation.

Maddie refilled both of their cups and set the carafe back on the warmer before sitting across from him. It was another warm and sunny day, a soft breeze blowing her red curls.

"What does it say?"

"Cause of death isn't a surprise. Strangulation with a scarf. Bibi's blood alcohol level was fairly high, point-one-five. Not falling down drunk but she was definitely impaired. To what extent I can't say. It would depend on her alcohol tolerance." Tanner tapped on a section of the paper. "Now this is interesting. She had old bruises on her body, mostly on her upper torso."

"Abuse?"

"That's a possibility. Because of the way they're clustered, the coroner has suggested that Bibi might have taken a fall. I'll mark that down as a question for friends and Leo, too." Tanner paged through the report. "Not much else. They took skin samples from under her nails for DNA analysis. She put up a fight. There may be more on the final report. This is only preliminary."

Tanner had specifically looked at Leo's hands and arms for wounds but hadn't seen any.

"So all they need is the results of the DNA test and they can tell who killed her? Easy-peasy."

Maddie made it sound like all they had to do was sit back and wait.

"Assuming they have a match in the system. If they can't get a warrant for Leo or anyone else's DNA they'll have to hope that the suspect volunteers their saliva."

"Why would a guilty person do that? That would be crazy."

"Exactly. That's why we still have to gather evidence. So we can get a judge to sign off on a warrant to compel the suspect to give a sample. Criminals aren't usually all that bright but they're not dumb as a rock, either."

"What about that guy that robbed the barbecue joint in Springwood? He sat down to eat some ribs and that's where you found him after he'd tripped the alarm."

Chuckling, Tanner recalled that particular break-in. The alarm had been silent and the robber had thought he'd have plenty of time to enjoy a nice meal before absconding with the cash.

"Okay, he wasn't all that bright. But most of them don't wander into the station and confess, offering up their DNA and fingerprints. It would be nice, though. It would make the job a hell of a lot easier."

"Did you tell the sheriff that Leo is planning to leave town?"

"I did when I talked to him last night. He didn't seem particularly concerned since like you, he thinks the entire case rests on the DNA evidence."

"Did you counsel him otherwise?"

"I may have given him some advice. That's what he wanted from me so that's what I gave him."

"How'd he take it?"

"Quite well. I have to say that Smith really seems to want to learn the job and be a good lawman. Unfortunately, he's going to have to learn it all the hard way. On the job training."

"So what's the plan for the day?"

Tanner eased out of his chair, coffee cup in hand. "First, I'm going to whip us up some breakfast. Then I'm going to talk to Randy and Carrie Knight. Separately. I've got the fun job of asking Randy if he was having an affair with Bibi. Then I get to ask Carrie if she'd heard the rumors about her husband."

"You're going to be about as popular as the plague," Maddie teased. "Way to win friends and influence people."

"I try and be sensitive but when a murder happens privacy is a thing of the past. They can hate me if it makes them feel better."

"I love you if it makes you feel any better."

It did, and it always had.

Chapter Sixteen

Randy Knight wasn't difficult to find. He was in the gym of the condo building, jogging on a treadmill, covered in sweat, earbuds in his ears. He gave Tanner a wave and then slowed down the machine, hopping off when it came to a halt.

"Hey, you're not exactly dressed for a workout," Randy joked, drinking down half a bottle of water. "I can lend you some exercise clothes if you wanted to lift. You can work in with me if you want."

"Not today, but thank you. Actually, I'm helping the sheriff with the investigation into Bibi's death. I was hoping I could ask you a few questions."

The easygoing smile fell from Randy's face. "It's not true."

"What's not true?"

Although Tanner had a decent idea what the other man was talking about.

"There are rumors running around town about me and Bibi but they weren't true. I love my wife."

Lots of men said that, but in Tanner's experience their idea of love and his were two different things.

"Why do you suppose people were saying you were having

an affair?"

Randy mopped his face with a towel. "Because we were friends. All four of us spent a lot of time together, going places and doing things. Let's face it. People love to gossip and if they can't find something to talk about, they'll make it up. Bibi was a good friend but that's all we were. I've never cheated on my wife."

Tanner would take the man at his word. Until there was solid evidence that said otherwise.

"According to the coroner's report, Bibi had bruises on her upper torso. Do you know where she might have got those?"

Randy nodded, looping the towel around his neck. "I sure do. Bibi was in a fender bender last week. She was rear ended by another car and her airbag went off. The other driver didn't stick around and took off."

Were the accident and the murder connected? Or just a coincidence?

"Did Bibi have any enemies? Anyone that would want to hurt her? Did she a disagreement with anyone recently?"

Will he mention Ashley?

"Not that I can think of. She was a sweet woman who wouldn't hurt a fly." Randy groaned and his head fell back for a moment before he continued. "Frankly, she could have done a hell of a lot better than Leo. I like the man and all but he was a less than stellar husband, if you know what I mean."

"Women? Gambling? Drinking?"

Those were the usual suspects when it came to marital disharmony.

"All three," Randy confirmed. "Leo can be the nicest guy in the world but when he drinks too much, he's a real asshole. As for women, he's not the biggest fan of monogamy and he doesn't make a secret of it."

"And the gambling?"

"He gets bored and he likes to bet on sports. I don't think he loses too much though and I've never heard Bibi give him a hard time about it. They lived separate lives to a certain extent. She had her interests and he had his."

"Was Leo seeing anyone recently?"

Tanner would need to talk to her. She had a motive for murder.

Randy's smile was grim. "Ashley. From what we could see she was vying to be the fourth Mrs. Leo Gordon."

Not exactly the most coveted position.

"Did Bibi know?"

"Of course, she did. Leo never bothered to hide it. As I said, he can be kind of a jerk. I might like going waterskiing with the guy but I sure as shit wouldn't want to be married to him."

"One more question?"

"Sure. Go ahead."

"Where were you at midnight yesterday?"

Randy's expression went blank, his smile gone in an instant. "At home. Asleep. You can ask my wife."

"I will. I ask these questions to rule out people one by one."

"I'll make it easy for you. I didn't kill Bibi. I really liked her."

"I appreciate your time. Let me know if you remember anything else."

Tanner turned to go but Randy stepped into his path. "Leo was talking about getting a divorce."

"They were unhappy?"

Randy shrugged. "They never seemed like it but Leo was prone to boredom. He said something about maybe getting a divorce a few months ago."

"Thank you, Randy. You've been very helpful."

Had Leo become impatient and decided that murder was

easier than a divorce? The husband was certainly still on the suspect list.

Next stop? Ashley Monroe.

✧ ✧ ✧ ✧

Maddie had wanted to accompany Tanner but he'd insisted that she keep her appointment at the spa. Under Sherry's close supervision, he'd set up a spa day for her that included a massage, a mani-pedi, and a facial. When he'd told her about it, she'd been thrilled, thinking it sounded like a day of heaven. But a hell of a lot had happened since then and she felt like she ought to be helping her husband catch a killer. He'd assured her that there would still be work to be done when she was finished.

The massage had put her in a relaxed mood despite all that was going on, so she was happily reading a glossy magazine while having her toes painted a bright fuchsia when Carrie sat down at the pedicure chair to her left.

So much for peace and serenity.

Carrie might have been smiling and welcoming that first night but now her expression looked like she'd just sucked on a lemon. She cast Maddie a nasty look and then angrily opened her own magazine, studiously avoiding any eye contact.

Okay. Fine. Tanner had warned her that they weren't going to make any friends during this investigation. It wasn't like they would see these people ever again once they left Florida.

Content not to rock the boat, Maddie kept her nose between the pages and ignored the woman next to her who was fussing and sighing every ten seconds.

"I hope you're happy."

Generally, yes.

But Maddie had a feeling that wasn't what Carrie was referring to.

Keeping her tone even, Maddie looked up from her magazine. "Excuse me?"

Carrie gave up reading, tossing the periodical onto an empty chair. "I said I hope you're happy."

I'm going to regret this. Tanner would tell me not to engage.

"About what, exactly?"

"Your husband sticking his nose into things that aren't his business," Carrie said through gritted teeth.

Her cheeks were red and she was almost shaking with anger.

Should I do this? Should I bother? What the hell…

For most of her life, Maddie had avoided conflict but she'd learned over the years that sometimes a person had to meet it head-on. She had a gut feeling that there was no way that Carrie was going to let Maddie out of this spa without a confrontation.

"Tanner is not sticking his nose into anything," Maddie responded, trying to sound patient when she wasn't. She'd had a great deal of practice as a doctor. "He was specifically asked for his help by the sheriff of this town. I would think as a friend of Bibi's you'd be glad that a well-respected, knowledgeable, and experienced lawman was assisting in the investigation to find her killer."

"He doesn't understand us," the other woman hissed, her gaze darting around the room. The only two other people were their aestheticians and while they were pretending that they weren't listening in…

They were definitely listening. If this town worked anything like Springwood, the gossip mill would have this all over by sundown.

"He doesn't understand you?" Maddie echoed, not even sure what that meant. "I wasn't aware that you needed understanding from a police officer when he's investigating a cold-blooded murder."

"He's not one of us," Carrie explained as if that cleared it all up. Far from it. "He should leave this to Sheriff Smith."

"Who has absolutely no experience with a murder case. Don't you want Bibi's killer to be brought to justice?"

Carrie turned her body toward Maddie, pulling her foot out of the manicurist's hands and sloshing water all over the floor. "Of course, I do. I loved Bibi like a sister."

"But she doesn't deserve a professional investigation?" Maddie challenged. "The killer isn't going to just walk into the sheriff's office and confess, you know. It doesn't work like that."

As I was reminded by my husband this morning.

"We don't need outsiders to help us. The sheriff can handle this."

"He says he can't," Maddie shot back. If she could have stomped away, she would have but her toe polish was still wet. "Tanner is helping where he can and that's it. I would think you all would be happy about that."

"Happy?" Carrie almost screeched the question. "You think I should be happy that he practically accused my husband of being a murderer?"

There was no way Tanner would have done that. He'd done this a time or two.

"I assume that Randy was asked to account for his whereabouts at the time of the murder?"

Carrie nodded, her lips pressed together in a mutinous line.

"Everyone has to account for their whereabouts, Carrie. Not just Randy. Everyone. Leo, Randy, Ashley, and…you, too."

The woman's eyes went round and if anything, she seemed to shake even more with rage.

"What about you?" she demanded. "Nothing ever happened in our town until you and your husband showed up. How do we know that you're not the killers?"

Maddie almost laughed but somehow kept her features under control. Carrie was certainly grasping at straws if she was accusing strangers of murdering Bibi.

"What motive would Tanner or I have?"

Shrugging, Carrie didn't answer immediately. "I don't know. You don't need a motive. Maybe you just like killing people."

"Tanner has caught one or two people like that. We're not one of them, though. I'm sorry that you're upset. I really am. But investigations by their very nature uncover secrets. Sending Tanner away isn't going to stop that from happening."

Carrie's fingers curled tightly around the arm of the chair, the knuckles white. "We don't have any secrets."

"Then you don't have anything to worry about," Maddie replied, her tone gentle. "But if you do—"

"No," Carrie interjected swiftly and firmly. "We don't have any secrets."

"Then it will all be okay."

Would it really? Carrie was extremely rattled, and not in an *innocent bystander* sort of way. Could she have snapped and murdered the other woman – Bibi? Did Carrie know that her husband had been with Bibi that night? She was afraid of something, that was for sure.

Maddie needed to talk to Tanner and find out what Randy Knight had said.

After talking to Randy, Tanner headed back upstairs but stopped in the lobby when he saw the concierge Brad at the desk. The young man was paid to keep an eye on people's comings and goings.

"Brad, how are you this morning?"

Brad greeted Tanner with a smile and a wave. "Really good,

Mr. Marks. How are you?"

"Doing well, thank you. And please call me Tanner."

"How can I help you today, Tanner? Restaurant reservation? Movie tickets?"

Tanner was about to say no but then paused, remembering that he and Maddie were on vacation. He was supposed to be romancing his wife, not finding a killer. She wasn't upset about it but he could do better.

"Actually, I'd like to find a great beach restaurant to surprise my wife. Someplace casual but has terrific food. Any suggestions?"

"I know just the place. They don't take reservations but this time of year you shouldn't have to wait for a table." Brad reached for a paper and pen. "I can draw you a map. It's just down the beach a few blocks."

Tanner probably didn't need a map to walk two or three blocks but he didn't want to hurt Brad's feelings. He did, however, want to talk to him about more than good food.

"Thanks, I appreciate that. I was also hoping you might answer a few questions for me. I'm not sure if you're aware but the sheriff asked me to help out on this murder investigation."

Looking up from his hand-drawn map, Brad frowned. "Why would he ask you to help? Are you a cop or something?"

Or something.

"Yes," Tanner replied, not going into detail. "I've solved a few murders in my career and this is your sheriff's first."

"What kind of questions do you want to ask me?"

Brad sounded guarded but he hadn't said no.

"Just a few simple ones. Have you seen anyone hanging around lately that shouldn't be here? Anyone out of place or acting strangely?"

Brad shook his head but then nodded. "Yes, there was this

one guy about a week ago. He was here to deliver a package and I told him he could leave it with me but he said no. He had to deliver it personally. I couldn't allow him upstairs, of course, and he got mad and stomped out."

Interesting.

"Who was he delivering the package to?"

"I don't know." Brad shrugged. "We didn't get that far in the conversation. He was really aggressive and kind of a jerk from the get-go. To be honest, he never should have gotten through the guard at the gate of the parking lot, but we have a new hire and sometimes he lets people through if they have a good story."

"Then the security guard would have his name and license plate? Do you remember the day and approximate time?"

"He should. Let's see…it was Wednesday and it was morning. Maybe ten or ten-thirty. I can't be exact."

"This is good and helpful." Tanner scribbled down the details in his little notebook. "Just a few more questions and we'll be done. Did you ever see Bibi Gordon arguing with anyone recently?"

Brad looked like he wanted to do just about anything but answer the question. He shuffled on his feet, his gaze darting all around the lobby and then settling on his shoes.

"I'm not sure I feel comfortable answering your question."

"I'll find out about whatever it is you're not telling me eventually," Tanner replied. "There's no such thing as a secret in a murder investigation, so you might as well say it."

The young man groaned and finally raised his head. "She argued with Leo."

Husbands and wives argue. Ninety-point-nine percent of the arguments didn't prove fatal.

"Did you hear what they were arguing about?"

Brad's cheeks turned a bright shade of red. "She accused him of having an affair."

"Did she say with whom?"

More clearing of the throat and stalling. Eventually he sighed, his shoulders slumping.

"Ashley Monroe."

Ms. Monroe was definitely on Tanner's list to talk to.

"Did you ever see Bibi with another man?"

"What? No. No way." Brad shook his head, his brows pinched together. "Not once."

"Do you only work days? Or have you worked any evenings?"

"I get off at six normally. Once a month I have to fill out a report for management so I might be here until six-thirty."

Then Brad wouldn't have any idea if Bibi made a habit of walking on the beach at night.

Tanner closed his notebook and tucked it in his pocket. "Thank you for answering my questions. Sometimes the smallest detail becomes the biggest break in the case."

Scraping his fingers through his short dark hair, Brad shook his head. "Are you going to tell Leo that I talked about their argument? I don't want to get in trouble."

"I won't tell him," Tanner assured the young man. "But if he gives you any trouble you need to let the sheriff know."

Brad promised he would and Tanner went upstairs, mentally gathering his to-do list. The most important item to be checked off?

Romancing the hell out of his beautiful wife.

CHAPTER SEVENTEEN

"A manda wants a dog."

Maddie had heard those words before from her own husband but so far, she'd successfully ignored them, delaying what was probably the inevitable.

While Tanner was questioning suspects, Maddie had decided to check in with home. Lounging on the couch, she'd studied her painted toes while Amanda had told her all about the fun she was having, and it totally included pretty much all the ice cream she could eat. But five-year-olds get bored quickly and she'd handed the phone over to Sherry after about five minutes to join the twins in a game of hide and seek.

"When did this come up?"

"So far? Every single day. She adores Bruno and he loves her. I think she might try and sneak him home in her little pink suitcase."

There was no way Bruno was going to fit. He was a huge yellow Lab and Sherry's first baby. Seriously, he thought he was a lap dog, climbing on Dan and Sherry when they were sitting on the couch or lying in bed. Maddie had actually witnessed with her own two eyes Dan cradling a full-grown Bruno in his arms like an infant.

"I hope you haven't been encouraging this."

Sherry loved dogs. Any dog. All shapes and sizes. When Tanner and Maddie had still had Scout the German Shepherd, she used to come over and play with him until Dan brought home Bruno the puppy.

"Why are you being so stubborn about this? You love dogs."

"Not as much as you."

"No one loves dogs as much as I do but I know that you love dogs, too. You spoiled the hell out of Scout when you thought no one was looking. Why do you pretend you're such a hard-ass when you're clearly not?"

Sighing, Maddie tried to think of a way to explain it to her friend without sounding like she'd lost her ever-loving mind. She barely understood it herself, but it was all part of this *world going too fast* issue she was having. At least now that she'd talked about it, it didn't seem so terrible or shameful.

"You know that I'd end up taking care of that dog. Amanda is too young."

"Are you saying that Tanner won't help out? Because I don't believe that for a second. He was Scout's primary caretaker."

"That's because Scout was really his dog."

Although Scout had been a retired police dog, Tanner would often take him into the station and let him socialize with the deputies. He didn't like the idea of Scout lying around the house bored all day long. Later when Scout got older and needed more rest, Tanner had relented, letting the canine snooze on a giant cushion most of the day.

Maddie could hear Sherry howling with laughter on the other end of the phone.

"You're afraid that the dog is going to attach to you and make you its person."

"I am not," Maddie defended. "It's just…"

"Just?" Sherry prompted. "Just what?"

"I'm just not sure I can go through it again. It was terrible the first time."

Silence.

"Did you hear me?"

"Yes, and I know what you mean. I just don't think about it that much."

"Ever?"

"I try not to. I just try and be in the moment with Bruno for however long we get to have him."

A lump took up residence in Maddie's throat, making it hard to speak.

"I'd love to have a dog, Sherry. But when I say that the world is moving too fast, I mean all of it. I'm not sure I can face that again. You put everything into caring for a dog, your heart and soul, and then one day…"

"You still don't get it. Nothing is forever, Maddie. You're so busy looking into the future you can't see that the now is going on right under your nose. You have to learn to live in the moment. Enjoy what you have. No one gets any guarantees about tomorrow. You're a doctor. You should know that."

"I think I'm in a weird state of denial."

"It won't make a bit of difference," Sherry stated. "I could try and be more gentle about this but life doesn't give a shit about your denial. It's going to keep going on and you're going to miss it. I'm begging you to stop and open your eyes."

A tear slid down Maddie's cheek and she rubbed at it with her knuckles.

"Tanner is older than I am."

There. There it was. The thing she'd been pushing so deep down inside of herself. The reality she hadn't wanted to even think about. So instead she'd concentrated on her own mortality. She'd distracted herself with Amanda growing up and the crow's feet that had appeared around her eyes. But sadly, that was a reminder that time was passing and it gave her no respite from that fear in the pit of her stomach.

"Yes, he is," Sherry replied, her tone gentle. "You knew that when you married him, and it's not like he has one foot in the grave and another on a banana peel. He's still pretty young and spritely. He's in great shape. He could live decades more. Hell, he might outlive us all."

"I love him so much," Maddie whispered, that ache in her heart that she'd been trying to keep at bay squeezing her ribs and making it hard to breathe. "I don't ever want to lose him."

"Wow, you really are going through a midlife crisis. Listen to me very closely. You're only forty, Tanner is only fifty-five, Amanda is five and parenting never ends. Even when she's thirty you'll be worrying about her and she'll be asking you for advice. By then you might even want a break."

"What if...I'm too happy?" The words were hard to say. "What if the universe thinks that I have too much good in my life and decides to take it all away?"

"Then you'll deal with it," Sherry replied immediately. "You're a strong woman, Maddie, and you'll be okay. There might be pain in the short term but in the long run you'll be fine."

"You sound so sure."

"Maddie, where is all of this coming from? It feels like it's come out of nowhere."

It had been coming for the last several months. Honestly? Since Maddie's *last* birthday.

"My mom," Maddie croaked, more tears falling down her cheeks. "She had it all too—"

She couldn't say anymore, her heart hurting far too much. Pain and fear had been building for too long.

"I know it's not rational," she said. "I know that it's crazy but here I am. Scared I'm going to lose it all. I don't make any sense whatsoever but I can't help but be frightened. Isn't that stupid? I've officially lost my mind. In my head I know that there's no real reason to be scared but I am."

"Emotions aren't always rational. I can understand why you would be scared. But you're not your mother. You're a separate human being and her fate is not yours."

"I know that. I really do. But I'm kind of freaked out about how quickly life is flying by. Tanner and I talked about it and we decided that I'd cut back on work and that made me feel better. It really did. At least for a while, but I can't help but feel swamped by fear. I'm just scared of losing it all. It could happen."

"A meteor could hit the earth and we could all perish. You can't live in fear. You have to face up to it. Yes, you're happy. And lucky. You're right that not everyone can say that. But it doesn't mean that the universe is waiting to drop a shoe. You might just have a great life."

"Luck. Fate. I feel powerless sometimes."

"Then take your power back. Live each day with gratitude. Live it like you won't get another. Tell Tanner how much you love him every single day. Hug and kiss Amanda. Listen to what the people in your life are really saying. And I mean really listen. Show them you care. Don't leave stuff on your bucket list undone. Slow down and enjoy life. Be present for it. Hell, that's some great advice there. I'm going to do it, too."

"Thank you, Dr. Sherry."

"You're welcome. Did I help?"

More than she would ever know. Just by being her friend.

"You did. I'm still a little scared but just talking about it has made me feel better."

"It always does." There was a small pause. "And Maddie? I get scared about all of that shit, too. You're not alone. Dan and I are so happy, and the twins are healthy. Everything is going so well and sometimes after everyone is in bed, I'll still be awake wondering if it could all be taken away from me."

I'm not alone. That does make me feel better.

"How do you handle it?"

"By getting up in the morning and living life with even more zest. Really dig into it. Because if you're busy thinking about all the worst-case scenarios you're definitely not enjoying your life."

"When did you get so wise, Dr. Sherry?"

"Would you believe I was born this way? Seriously, your fears are common but don't let that boogeyman run your life. Fight back. You and Tanner have a lot of living left to do. Just don't waste your time. And get your daughter a dog. You know you want one, too."

To be honest? Maddie did.

CHAPTER EIGHTEEN

Tanner was up to something. Ten years ago, Maddie wouldn't have realized it but she'd been married to him long enough to know when he had something up his sleeve. He loved to surprise her even when it was something silly like making her favorite dinner or a foot massage when she was tired after a long day. There had never been a brand-new car in the driveway with a big red bow like in those commercials – thank goodness – but she was a woman who appreciated his tokens of love. Years ago, Sherry had said that Tanner wouldn't be a man that talked about how much he loved her—he'd show her instead.

Sherry was a wise woman.

So she could tell by the way he kept moving her from room to room in the condo, then disappearing to "take a walk", and then finally urging her to relax in the tub. They were supposed to go out to dinner on Friday night for her birthday so it couldn't be that...

Clean from head to toe – thanks to a tub full of bubbles – and dressed casually in a sundress with minimal makeup, Maddie walked hand in hand with Tanner to the restaurant he'd chosen for dinner. This must be the surprise because she could barely keep up with his long legs. He was damned eager to get to their destination.

He'd showered as well and he smelled incredibly good. It was one of the first things that had attracted her to him when they'd met as adults. Okay, his stunning looks and physique hadn't hurt. Nor had his caring and respectful nature. He'd been head and shoulders over any other man she'd ever dated, so it hadn't been a stretch to find herself falling ass over tea kettle for him in a short amount of time.

It was a lovely night, warm but not too humid. Maddie could smell the salt in the air mixed with a floral scent that she couldn't identify. The sky was turning pink and purple as the day drew to a close. Since talking to Sherry earlier, a sense of calm had come over Maddie that she hadn't had in quite a long time. Her friend was right. As usual.

There wasn't a way to slow down time, but she could embrace each day and moment with as much fervor as Sherry did. The true tragedy would be not living this life she had been given because she was so worried about...everything. She had so much. Instead of worrying about losing it she needed to jump in with both feet and savor it. The answer to her problems was so simple and yet she'd completely overlooked it. That's how deep in her own issues she'd been. For someone that prided herself on being practical and open, she'd dropped the ball completely.

"I hope you like this place. Brad highly recommended it."

"You talked to Brad?"

"He did say he was the resident expert regarding the local cuisine."

"I'm sure I'll love it." She gave Tanner's hand a squeeze. "I love you."

His smile widened and he pulled her closer, his arm around

her waist. Nothing too risqué since they were walking on a public street, though.

"I love you, too. Did I mention that you seem really happy tonight?"

"You didn't but I am. And why wouldn't I be? I'm here with my favorite guy in a semitropical paradise. It's all good."

"Even though I'm working a little, too?"

"I told you it's fine. It's all fine. I spent a nice afternoon at the pool. And I talked to Sherry and Amanda, too."

Tanner had called their daughter before they'd left for dinner to say goodnight.

"That's great. She says she loves school and she's eating a lot of ice cream."

"Sherry says that Amanda wants a dog." Maddie took a deep breath. "I'm thinking that when we get back home, we should start looking for one."

Tanner stopped on the sidewalk, his brows almost to his hairline. "Wait…are you saying yes to a dog? I thought you didn't want one."

She could have gone into all the reasons she'd thought she shouldn't have one but did Tanner really want to hear it all?

"I think that Amanda is at a good age for a dog," she said. "And I know that I won't end up doing all the work because you'll do it, too."

"Of course, I will. This is terrific. Amanda is going to be so excited."

He wasn't fooling anyone.

"You're excited too."

Now she felt kind of like shit because he'd clearly wanted a dog more than she'd realized. He was grinning like he'd won the lottery and a lifetime supply of steak and ice cream.

"I guess I am. It will be fun to have a puppy around the

house again." Laughing, he leaned down and dropped a kiss on her brow. "Don't worry. I'll protect your shoes."

"I'm not worried about my shoes. At least not all of them. My black leather pumps were expensive, though."

Maddie didn't know much about clothes and shoes. Sherry had made her buy those pumps and she had to admit they'd been a good investment. She'd worn them many times and they were extremely comfortable.

"We just need to remember to keep the closet closed." His finger slipped up down her bare arm, sending tingles to her toes. "Baby, I'm not complaining or anything so don't think that I am. I'm thrilled that you're open to getting a dog, but I can't help but wonder what changed your mind."

"Dr. Sherry," Maddie admitted. "She and I had a good talk this afternoon."

"That's great. Can I ask what about? Maybe she could hang out a shingle."

"She is good at giving advice—after all she decided that I should marry you before I did. We did talk and I admitted that I was frightened about losing everything. I feel so lucky and I know that it could all be gone in an instant. I got scared and I guess I'd spiraled down to the point that I couldn't see that I was missing out on actually living this great life that I'd been given. She gave me a hand out of the dark, you could say."

"You could have talked to me."

There was hurt in his tone and she'd put it there. She wasn't proud of not talking to her husband. Normally she and Tanner had an open and honest relationship, but this one time...

"You seemed like you had a lot on your own plate."

It was several beats before he answered.

"I guess I did but I don't think it's healthy that we weren't talking to each other. Where did we lose our way?"

"I'm not sure. Life gets busy and crazy and I think we were just trying to survive it. We were both in the quagmire and I think we didn't want to make it worse for the other."

"Just so you know, you could never make it worse for me. I want to know what's bothering you, Maddie."

"I want to know what's bugging you, too." Giggling, she linked her arm with his. "You can dump all of your problems on me anytime."

His expression relaxed, his entire demeanor more at ease. "Good to know. I feel the same. Now how about we have some dinner and enjoy ourselves? I have plans for you."

A shiver ran down her spine at his tone. His plans were always so delightfully wicked.

Sherry had encouraged Maddie to embrace life fully. No better time to start that than right now.

Brad had been right on the money with his restaurant recommendation. Their dinner had been delicious and Maddie had enjoyed every single bite of the buttery lobster tail. Tanner had steak with his lobster tail but they'd both saved room for dessert – a decadent chocolate mousse that tasted bitter and sweet on her tongue at the same time. She didn't even think about the calories, instead savoring each smooth and creamy spoonful. If this was embracing life, she was all for it.

They'd walked hand in hand back to the condo, the warm breeze keeping the humidity from being completely oppressive. It had rained for a short time while they were eating and the dampness hung in the air. She was giggling as Tanner unlocked their door.

"What is so funny? You look quite tickled."

Slapping a hand over her mouth, she shook her head.

"I shouldn't tell you."

Tanner's eyes were twinkling, enjoying her merriment even if he wasn't in on the joke.

"You definitely should. I'd like a good laugh, too."

Why not?

"Moist."

His forehead furrowed in confusion. "What? I don't get it."

"Outside." She waved an arm towards the windows. "After the rain, it was moist outside. I couldn't think of any other word but you know how I hate that word. Sherry hates it too, unless you're talking about cake."

"Moist," Tanner repeated dutifully. "I didn't know you hated that word. What's wrong with it?"

"It's…kind of icky."

"Icky? You're being pretty hard on a single word. It's just a word. I think this is your dirty mind working overtime here."

"Then say it," she demanded with a smile. "Say it several times and then tell me what you think."

Rolling his eyes, he humored her, repeating the word half a dozen times.

"And?"

"Okay, I see what you mean. But you were right, it was…moist outside."

She fell back onto the couch cushions. "I'm not making this stuff up."

"Really? I'm making it all up as I go along." He waggled his brows like an evil villain in an old black and white movie. "Since we got all sweaty…and moist, you want to take a shower? And get…wet?"

She looked up at him from under her lashes. "Will you wash my back?"

"Honey, I'll not only wash it, I'll kiss every inch of it."

"Then let's do this."

Yes, the romance had changed in the last ten years. Less candlelight and soft music but much more love and passion. She was amazed that Tanner could still make her tingle and swoon after all of this time, but if anything, he was far more potent now. He knew all the places that sent her into orbit and he made a point of making sure he hit all the hot spots.

Maddie stripped down while Tanner adjusted the temperature of the water. Somehow, he'd already managed to get naked and she had to marvel at how quickly he'd done it. She'd barely blinked and his clothes were gone. But that meant that she could leisurely admire his physique, lean and hard. Because of the grueling physical nature of his job, Tanner had always been careful to work out regularly and keep himself in top shape, although he'd complained lately that it was getting more difficult.

"Like what you see?"

Oops, she'd been caught staring.

But who can blame me?

"I certainly do."

His arm snaked out and pulled Maddie flush against his body. "I like what I see too, honey."

Capturing her lips with his, he helped her step into the large tiled shower and closed the door behind them. Water cascaded down her back and she leaned into the stream, letting the heat chase away her tension. Tanner's large hands were massaging her neck and shoulders, the soap dripping down. He worked those muscles until she was groaning with pleasure, her eyes drifting closed. He worked his way down her back and legs before lifting her hands and pressing them against the wet tile wall.

"Brace yourself here."

Those too clever hands were now reaching around her and working on her front, his rough palms cupping her breasts and pinching the nipples. If she hadn't been holding herself up again the wall, her knees would have given out. Her pulse quickened and her arousal built as Tanner ever so slowly worked over her belly and then finally down to her slit.

His left arm wrapped around her torso to keep her upright as the fingers on his right hand delved between her legs, unerringly finding her clit, already swollen and needy.

"Tanner," she breathed, but for the life of her she couldn't think of anything she wanted to say except that she needed more. More of him. Preferably right away.

The temperature in the shower seemed to have risen, the steam wrapping around them and playing a game of hide and seek. Maddie rested her head back on Tanner's chest as his deft fingers drove her closer and closer to her climax. He took his time, not a bit in a hurry, content to let her arousal build slowly. The tension grew in Maddie's abdomen, coiling tighter and tighter with each stroke on her clit. It was excruciating and pure pleasure all at the same time, waiting for what would surely be a cataclysmic explosion.

"Are you with me, honey?" His lips were close to her ear, his voice like gravel. "Can you come for me now? Are you ready?"

It was all too much. The feel of Tanner's breath on her cheek. The timbre of his voice sending shivers up her spine. The sensation of the water sluicing off of her sensitive skin. His knowledgeable fingers making a mockery of any control Maddie might have still had.

That coil in her belly tightened painfully one more time before springing free, her orgasm sending her reeling as if she'd been hit by a freight train. Flames ran through her veins and sparks exploded behind her eyelids as she clung to Tanner like a lifeline. If he'd let go of her, she would have fallen into a heap on the tile floor.

Before her climax was even done, Tanner hefted her up in his arms and turned her around so her back was pressed against the wall. Lifting her legs, he impaled himself deeply inside of her in one deliciously delightful stroke. She wrapped her legs around his lean middle, her fingers clenching his damp shoulders. He was grunting with each hard thrust, his cock rubbing all the sensitive spots inside of her.

She would have a few bruises tomorrow on her hips from where he was holding her so firmly but right now, she didn't care in the least. Pulling his head down, her fingers scraping through his wet, silky hair, she whispered filthy, dirty words into his ear, exhorting him to fuck her harder and faster. Give her his cock and make her beg. She'd learned that he liked his dirty talk so she gave it to him in spades. It spurred her arousal on as well, and she was surprised to find herself building toward another release despite having come only minutes before.

"Give it to me," she urged, her voice choked as he sucked on her neck. She'd have a mark there, too. "Fuck me hard."

His face was beautiful and tortured at the same time, his teeth snapped together and bared like a wild animal. He was riding her hard and giving her everything that she was begging for and then some. She whimpered as she teetered on the edge of the precipice once more, not sure if she would survive the second fall.

"Come," he commanded. "Come now."

It was all she needed to go tumbling into the abyss, whirling around until she was dizzy, her soul shattering into a million pieces and then slowly coming back together as she drifted down from her high. At some point Tanner had reached his peak as well, his arms clamped around her like steel bands.

It wasn't until she could keep her eyes open without the world tilting on its axis that Tanner cautiously allowed her toes to touch the shower floor. Even then, he held her protectively, his large body shielding hers until she could stand on her own.

"Getting clean has never been so much fun," Tanner said with a chuckle and a kiss to her lips. "I think we're going to sleep well tonight."

They might even sleep past sunrise. Together.

CHAPTER NINETEEN

Tanner didn't want to get out of bed early the next morning but Sheriff Ken Smith was stopping by for a discussion about the ongoing investigation. He felt slightly more awake and human after a quick shower – alone this time – and a cup of coffee but he was still yawning when he opened the door to the younger man.

"I'm sorry about the early hour," Ken said, taking a seat at the kitchen table. Tanner had poured him a cup of coffee. "I have a meeting with the town council after this and they're all over me to get this murder solved so it's out of the papers. They say it's bad for tourism, which is basically the only industry we have in our town."

Tanner had had many a meeting with the various mayors of Springwood through the years. Most of them had been fine but a few had been downright unpleasant. Like the last one with Pete.

"It's not a problem. We just need to keep it down because my wife is still sleeping."

Maddie didn't sleep late much but he was glad she was getting a chance to do just that. When he'd closed the bedroom door behind him she was still asleep, her hair like a halo on the pillow. She'd looked so peaceful and serene.

"No problem. I just wanted to say again that I'm grateful as hell for the help. I have the backing of the town council on this too, although we have no money to pay—"

"Don't worry about that," Tanner cut in. "I'm not doing this for money. I'm doing it to help you out."

"I still can't believe you're helping me."

"I'm hopefully *teaching* you as well. It's great that you haven't had anything bad happen here but you can't count on that continuing after this. Now you'll know what to do."

The younger man's head nodded vigorously. "I am absolutely learning from you. I'm getting more of an idea of what I need to do."

"That's good." Tanner took a sip of his coffee. "I'm not sure if you're aware but Leo is planning to leave Florida in a few days. He's going to visit some friends in New York City."

Ken's eyes widened. "That's not good, right? Can I stop him? Should I stop him? I mean…do we think he's guilty?"

It was an excellent question. One that Tanner didn't yet have an answer for.

"I don't know," he answered honestly. "I think Leo Gordon is still a viable suspect and I'm not that concerned if all he's doing is going to New York City. Now if he's planning to leave the country from there, that's an issue. As for whether you can stop him, not really. You can ask him to delay his trip but he can say no."

"The DNA from Bibi's fingernails won't be back for weeks," Ken lamented. "I doubt I can keep him here that long if he's determined to leave."

Rubbing his chin, Tanner assessed the options. "It might not work but you could have the coroner not release the body. That will sometimes keep your suspect in the area. Not weeks, but maybe for a few extra days."

"I can try that. Have you had a chance to talk to Ashley Monroe yet?"

"I knocked on her door a few times yesterday but she didn't answer. We might have to make that conversation more official in the sheriff's station." Sometimes a person needed to have their world shook up a little before they took the situation seriously. "We also need to talk to Leo again. Maybe this time in the station as well."

Wincing, Ken cleared his throat. "He's all lawyered up. I got a call from his attorney that said any questions should be submitted in writing through him."

"Fine, let's start compiling them. You don't want him thinking that he runs this investigation. You need to keep the pressure on."

"Right, right." Ken ducked his head and shifted in his chair. "I know you're not going to be happy but I'm having trouble getting footage from the security cameras up and down the beach. A few people have been accommodating, but some don't want to do it and they said that I need to get a warrant. Should I do that?"

"Not yet," Tanner responded. "Let's look at the video that we have and see if we need any more. Also, is there a red light camera at the traffic light near the condo? If so, see if you can get that footage. We might get lucky."

They chatted for a few more minutes before Ken left, thanking Tanner once again for the help. The guy looked like he wanted to do just about anything but go to that meeting with the town council.

Whistling, Tanner headed into the kitchen to make breakfast for Maddie. The scent of food always woke her up. He shouldn't be so damn happy that he wasn't the poor bastard that had to go to that meeting but he was. Getting fired might have been the best thing that had ever happened to him.

It was after breakfast and Maddie and Tanner were relaxing on the sunny patio when Logan called. Tanner put the phone on speaker so she could hear the conversation, too.

"Enjoying the warm weather?" Logan asked with a laugh. "It's cold as hell here."

"Then maybe it's time to take Ava on a vacation," Maddie teased. "I bet she would love it."

"She would," he agreed. "But right now, she's on a deadline for a new book. Maybe after the first of the year. She always says the months after the holidays but before spring are the worst."

Maddie couldn't agree more. She had vivid memories of a few Chicago winters that seemed like they'd last forever.

"So what have you got for us?" Tanner asked, placing the cell phone on the table between them. "Any good news?"

"Depends on what you might call good news. First, I ran the license plate of the guy with the package from last week. He checked out clean. He wanted to leave a gift for his ex-girlfriend who was staying with a friend. She'd told him to leave her alone but apparently he's not a good listener. I don't think he has anything to do with your case."

"I also checked out the finances of Randy and Carrie Knight, plus Leo Gordon a little more closely. Seems that Randy Knight's business received an influx of cash about four months ago. From whom, you might wonder? Leo Gordon. I don't know about you but I don't usually hand out huge swaths of cash to men that are supposedly having an affair with my wife."

That was an understatement on Logan's part.

"I would imagine that any man that you thought was having

an affair with Ava would be six feet under," Maddie replied. "And you'd make it look like an accident."

"So would she if the roles were reversed," Logan laughed. "Ava can be quite bloodthirsty. But the influx of capital into Knight's business isn't the interesting part. I dug more deeply into Leo Gordon's finances and look what I found. The other woman."

"Ashley Monroe?" Tanner asked, giving Maddie a quick nod. "According to Knight, she's the next Mrs. Leo Gordon."

"Nope. There's another woman in Gordon's life and he's spending money hand over fist on her. Definitely a man courting a female."

"How can you tell?" Maddie asked.

"I don't buy my friends jewelry and lingerie," Logan said. "Plus perfume, expensive dinners, and various and sundry gifts. Trust me. He might be sleeping with this Ashley Monroe but she's not the next on deck."

"What did you find about Ashley Monroe?" Tanner queried. "Anything interesting?"

"Not really. She's been married twice, both times to rich men. She received generous settlements and she lives within her means. She's made some excellent investments and has a diverse portfolio. She's rich by most people's standards but not wealthy. From what I can see her major vice is obscenely expensive shoes. She has lots of friends and socializes a great deal. If she wants to level up and catch an even wealthier husband, she shouldn't have a problem. She runs in the right circles. She has no major debt, no skeletons in the closet. She's basically an open book. What you see is what you get. We like those types in this business. My gut tells me that she's not your killer."

Logan was an instinctual lawman and everyone respected that little voice inside of him.

"It's good to be able to knock someone off of the suspect list," Tanner said. "I'm thinking the same as you. Ashley Monroe doesn't strike me as the murdering type, although I'd still love to talk to her. So far, she's been making that difficult. She can't be found."

"I can put a track on her credit cards. Let you know the next time she uses them."

"I don't think we need to do that. Yet. The local sheriff left his card on her door this morning. That should let her know that we're serious about talking to her. If she still doesn't contact us, then I'll let you know. Did you get any details about Gordon's first marriage?"

"I did and it's about what we expected. Rocky marriage. My source says that the wife contacted a divorce attorney before she died but she didn't get a chance to file. Gordon was questioned by the police but he had an alibi."

"I hope it's a better one than the one he has now," Tanner groused. "Upstairs asleep isn't exactly ironclad."

"It's about as lame. He was hanging out at a buddy's house drinking. The friend confirmed it. The investigation was eventually dropped when no other leads came up."

"How convenient," Maddie muttered under her breath. "One friend alibis the other."

"I want to talk to that friend," Tanner said. "Think you can find out who he is and find him? I also want to talk to Gordon's lady friend. If she was going to be the next wife, she did have a vested interest in ending his marriage. One way or the other."

"I'm sending you all her info via email. As for the identity of Gordon's alibi, I'll keep working on that." A small pause. "Are you having fun working on the case? Because we have about a dozen more backed up here that we could use a hand with."

Maddie's gaze traveled from the phone to Tanner, who appeared to be visibly uncomfortable. They hadn't talked much about his future since their last conversation. She didn't want to push him in any direction. She only wanted him to be happy.

"I wouldn't call it fun," Tanner finally replied. "Especially since I'm supposed to be on vacation getting a break from work. We'll talk about this more when I get back home."

His tone was firm and Logan must have picked up on it even through the phone, because their friend dropped the subject altogether.

"I'll give you a call when I get more information. Just be careful, okay? You've got a killer running loose down there and I'm betting they don't want to be caught."

An ominous warning on a bright, sunny day. She'd make sure Tanner didn't take any crazy chances. If he didn't watch his back, she'd give him a bit of help.

CHAPTER TWENTY

Tanner had the sheriff set up their meeting with Leo's girlfriend Dina Wallace. Ken couldn't make it but Maddie had jumped at the chance to go. Her husband hadn't been all that enthused by the idea but she'd pointed out that Ava and Presley would have been allowed to go and he'd reluctantly given in. All while muttering...

"I'm going to have a talk with Seth and Logan."

"Maybe I want to learn more about what you do," Maddie had said during the drive in their rental car to Dina Wallace's home in a nearby city. "You should take it as a compliment."

"I would but I don't do this anymore. Technically speaking. You've never shown much interest in policework before."

"Now that's not true," she protested. "When we were first dating you took me to that murder crime scene and I found that discarded coffee cup. Remember?"

"No."

She didn't believe him for a second. Tanner had an amazing memory.

"Yes, you do. You absolutely remember. You probably remember better than I do."

"I remember that I sent you home as quickly as possible. You shouldn't be hanging around grisly crime scenes."

Sometimes her husband said the funniest things. She had to laugh out loud at this one. She'd worked in one of the busiest – and bloodiest – emergency rooms in Chicago. Some bloody abandoned building wasn't going to give her nightmares.

"I think you've conveniently forgotten what I do for a living, husband."

"I think you've conveniently forgotten that cop work can be dangerous...wife. There's a killer on the loose if you haven't noticed."

She batted her eyelashes at him. "I feel very safe with you. Besides, I can help you with questioning Dina Wallace. I can be watching her expressions and body language while you concentrate on her answers."

She had him. His lips were twisted as if he wanted to say that she was wrong but he couldn't bring himself to lie.

Sighing, he nodded in agreement. "Having you there will hopefully relax her a bit. Get her thinking that this isn't nearly as official as bringing her into the station would be. She might lower her defenses."

"So she's definitely a suspect?"

"She had motive, although how strong it is could be debated. Now it's time to see if she had opportunity and means. As I've mentioned before, I'm not leaning toward a female killer. It would have taken a great deal of strength to overpower Bibi and strangle her."

The city that Dina lived in was mid-sized at about a hundred thousand residents. She didn't live on the beach but in a villa community inland. It was a charming neighborhood with Spanish-style homes and lots of palm trees. They easily found her unit and parked in front.

"Now let me do most of the talking," Tanner said as they approached the door. "You're here to watch her. Also, get a good look at her surroundings such as photos or memorabilia. It might tell us something about Leo that we didn't know."

"Gotcha."

Maddie had always considered herself observant. In her job she had to be. This was simply a different form of observation.

The door flew open before they even had a chance to knock on it. Dina Wallace must have been waiting for them.

"Please come in," she said, stepping back to they could enter. "Can I get you something to drink? It's really hot out there today."

From what Maddie had experienced since arriving in Florida, it was hot out there every single day this time of the year.

They said no thank you and were ushered into the living room. The villa wasn't huge but it was meticulously maintained inside and out and decorated beautifully. The living room and kitchen, which was really one big room, was done in tan and red with splashes of blue and green here and there. If Maddie lived to a hundred and twenty, she'd never be able to pull something like this off. She kept her own wardrobe simple for this very reason and she'd had Sherry help pick out the furnishings in her own home.

"Thank you so much for seeing us on such short notice," Tanner said, settling onto the couch. "We appreciate your cooperation with this investigation."

"Of course, I'll do anything to help Leo find out who killed Bibi."

I wonder if she realizes that what she says may not help Leo?

Now that they were sitting across from Dina, Maddie was able to get a better look at their hostess. Dina was young.

Really young.

If she was thirty, Maddie was a monkey's uncle. Now, far be it for her to be judgey about age differences in couples...there were fifteen years between herself and Tanner, after all. But Leo had to be at least sixty and this young woman looked to be in her late twenties.

Blonde, blue-eyed, and petite, Dina was the opposite of Bibi looks-wise, although both of them seemed to have an open smiling attitude when it came to strangers.

Maddie let her gaze wander around the room. "You have a beautiful home, Ms. Wallace. Really lovely."

"Thank you so much." Dina's smile widened, showing perfectly white and straight teeth. "I'm an interior decorator, actually."

It made Maddie feel slightly better that a real professional had decorated this home and not an amateur.

Tanner had his little notebook out and his pencil was already taking down notes. They'd barely said anything.

"How did you meet Leo Gordon, Ms. Wallace?"

"Please, I hope you both will call me Dina. I met Leo and Bibi when I did a decorating job for them. They wanted Leo's office redone and reorganized."

"How long ago was that?"

"About nine months ago. Right after New Year's. They were such a wonderful, welcoming couple. You couldn't help but love them. I can't believe this has happened. It's so awful. So very terrible."

Dina's lips trembled and her chin wobbled but she only sniffled a few times, controlling her tears.

"How well would you say you knew Leo and Bibi?"

Dina sat back in the chair and casually crossed her legs. "Pretty well. I mean...we're friends."

It was interesting. Watching someone lie. It had happened to

Maddie, of course, but not in the context of a murder investigation.

Tanner shot Maddie a quick glance before continuing his questioning.

"Do you know of anyone who might have wanted to hurt Bibi? Anyone she was arguing with, perhaps?"

"No, not at all. Everyone adored Bibi. I can't imagine who would want to hurt her like that."

Hurt must be the designated euphemism for kill in this conversation.

"When was the last time you saw Bibi?"

Dina shifted in her chair, looking uncomfortable. "I think it was a few weeks ago."

"Can you be more specific?"

The young woman frowned at Tanner's question. "Is it important?"

"It is, yes."

"It was two and a half weeks ago. Leo and Bibi had a party."

"Thank you." Tanner scribbled down more in the notebook. Just what was he writing, anyway? Was he actually taking notes or pretending in order to unnerve his suspects? Maddie was leaning toward the latter.

"Now, Ms. Wallace–"

"Dina," she interjected. "Call me Dina."

"Dina," Tanner repeated dutifully. "Can you tell me where you were the night of Bibi Gordon's death? Around midnight?"

Dina's shoulders stiffened. "Am I a suspect?"

"It's standard procedure to rule out people that knew the deceased."

"Then you should know that I was in bed at midnight. I would expect that's the answer you're going to get from most people."

"You're correct. Most people are in bed." Tanner leaned forward, his elbows on his knees. "Can you tell me how long you and Leo Gordon have been romantically involved?"

Her eyes went round and her mouth fell open. She appeared to be trying to form an answer but was too angry to do so, if the color on her cheeks was any indication.

"How dare you," she said between gritted teeth. "Leo Gordon is a married man."

"Yes, he is," Tanner agreed. "And I apologize if I'm out of line but I don't think that I am, Ms. Wallace. You were the recipient of many gifts—"

"Friendly gifts," Dina said. "Gifts between friends. Nothing more."

Tanner flipped to a page near the back of his notebook. "Diamond earrings, a diamond necklace, a diamond and sapphire bracelet, a half dozen sets of lingerie, three bottles of perfume, a designer gown and Christian Louboutin shoes, a weekend at a spa—"

"Stop," Dina begged loudly. "Just stop. How do you know all of that?"

Really? Had Dina Wallace been living under a bridge these last few years? Nothing was a secret anymore. And certainly not purchases that Leo Gordon had made with a credit card. Add in Dina's own social media accounts and anyone could have made the connection.

"It's my job to know all of this," Tanner responded patiently. Maddie had to admire that there was no judgment in his expression. Simple curiosity, that was all. "And modern technology certainly helps. We can play this game and pretend that you two weren't involved, but there are photos of the two of you together at a cafe in Paris and a chalet in Switzerland."

The air seemed to leak out of Dina, and she slumped against

the chair cushion. "It's not like you think it is. Leo and I are in love."

Then it's exactly like we think it is.

"Did Bibi know about you and Leo?" Tanner asked.

"I don't know," Dina admitted. "Leo was planning to tell her and ask for a divorce so we could be together. He said he wanted it to be a civilized matter. He didn't want it to be ugly or nasty."

Murder was ugly. Nasty, too.

"But I doubt Bibi would have cared about Leo and me," Dina went on. "She and Randy Knight were having an affair. Leo and I saw her and Randy on the beach one night. Their marriage was basically over long before me."

Way to rationalize it.

"But Leo hadn't told her yet?"

"Not that I know of. All of this happened…" Her voice trailed off and she buried her face in her hands. "I really cared about Bibi. She was a good person and she didn't deserve this."

Maddie couldn't stay quiet. "No one deserves to be murdered in cold blood."

Dina nodded and reached for a tissue. "She was such a good friend and everyone is going to miss her."

I don't think I would count the woman who was screwing my husband as a friend.

"Were you at the wake for Bibi?" Tanner asked. "I don't think I saw you there."

"I had an out-of-town client," Dina explained. "I couldn't make it."

Tanner flipped to another page in his notebook.

"Dina, were you aware that Bibi was Leo Gordon's third wife?"

The young woman shook her head. "No, you're wrong. Bibi

was his second wife."

"Actually, she was his third," Tanner replied, his tone firm. "His first wife Caroline drowned in their swimming pool. Let me ask you, Dina, what do you think the odds are of having two wives die so young? Caroline wasn't even twenty-five and Bibi was only thirty-five."

Dina's face had gone pale, all the color drained from her skin. She was still shaking her head in denial.

"You have to be wrong. Leo would have told me if something like that had happened to him. He would have told me."

"He's not wrong," Maddie said softly, leaning forward so Dina could hear her. "His first wife was supposedly walking in her sleep and she got tangled in her nightgown."

"Supposedly?" Dina's gaze flickered between Tanner and Maddie. "Are there some questions about that?"

"Leo was questioned by the police," Tanner replied. "They deemed the death suspicious but they couldn't prove anything. He had an alibi. He was at a friend's house drinking."

Visibly shaken, the young woman stood and began to pace the small space between the chair and the dining table. "You must be mistaken. It's some sort of case of mistaken identity. Leo would have told me."

"I can't comment on whether he would or not. All I can say is that my information is solid. Bibi was Gordon's third wife, not second. Hell of a run of bad luck for one man to have. It's not unheard of, but it does beg to have a few questions asked, don't you think?"

Dina stopped, her expression determined. "I'll just ask him about it. I'm sure there's a reason he didn't say anything. It's probably a terribly painful memory for him to talk about."

Tanner tucked his notebook into his pocket and pulled out a business card, laying it face up on the coffee table between them.

"I imagine that it is. Thank you for your time today. If you think of anything that might be helpful give me a call. That's my cell number. I'll be in town through the weekend and after that you can call the sheriff directly. I've written his number on the back of the card."

Picking up the card, Dina flipped it over, a frown on her face. "Where will you be?"

Levering to his feet, Tanner held out his hand to Maddie. "I'm working with the sheriff's department on a consulting basis. I don't live in Florida. I live in Montana."

They walked to their vehicle, Maddie also thanking Dina for her time on the way. They'd given the young woman a great deal to think about after they were gone. Whether Leo Gordon was innocent or guilty, he was definitely shady. Dina might want to rethink her relationship.

As they drove away, Tanner glanced over his shoulder at the neighborhood disappearing into the distance.

"I guarantee you she's on the phone to Gordon right now."

He was probably right. He usually was and it was annoying as hell.

"Do you think she had anything to do with Bibi's death?"

Tanner flashed a grin and chuckled. "No, but she might be ready to kill Gordon, or at least neuter him. Under all of that bravado, she's mad about being blindsided. I wouldn't want to be him, if you know what I mean."

"This sort of feels like it was a waste of time," Maddie lamented. "We don't know anything more than we did before we talked to her."

"That's not true. We know that she didn't know about Caroline, the first wife. We know what her story is for the time of the murder. I can verify it by checking the traffic camera on the corner of her neighborhood. One way in and one way out.

Convenient for me. But I didn't get a feeling that she's involved with this. I think she's just one more innocent caught up with Gordon."

"So you think he murdered Bibi?"

"I think that he needs further investigating. I'm not ruling him out at all. By the time we get home, Logan should have emailed all of that background on Gordon and Knight. We need to comb through it carefully. We should also have the camera footage to go through. Hopefully we'll know more after that."

Did Leo Gordon kill his wife? Or was it Randy Knight? Or Carrie? Or someone completely unrelated? So many questions and few answers. Somewhere they needed to catch a break or a murderer was going to go free.

CHAPTER TWENTY-ONE

O n the way home, Tanner and Maddie picked up some takeout food to feed their growling stomachs. He'd handed Maddie the key while he juggled two bags of piping hot food when he heard a noise on the other side of the condo door.

There shouldn't be anyone inside their unit.

His heart sped up in his chest and he wished dearly that he had more of a weapon than an order of lasagna and a dozen garlic knots. Shoving one of the bags into his other arm, he raised his hand and lightly pressed it over Maddie's lips. She gave him a startled glance but seemed to trust him enough not to question his action out loud. He nodded toward the door and then placed the bags on the floor before taking the key from her fingers.

So what's the plan?

I don't know. We're surprising him, that's for sure.

You don't have a weapon.

I know and that's an issue.

He looped an arm around Maddie's waist and pushed her behind him, his ears straining to hear what was happening on the other side of the door. He could hear movement and perhaps the sound of cabinets or closets being opened or closed. Was their visitor looking for something?

Adrenaline surging, Tanner pictured the entryway of the condo, looking for any possible weapon to use against the intruder. There were a few pictures on the wall, a table with a mirror over it, and a small brass vase holding a bouquet of silk flowers.

Bingo. The vase it would have to be. He'd made due with less a few times in the past but he couldn't recall being all that successful, to be honest. Turning around, he whispered in Maddie's ear.

"Stay here. Don't move until I say it's safe."

Her eyes widened and he could easily see that she wanted to object, but he shook his head again.

"I don't want to have to worry about both you and him. Promise me."

Her cheeks were pink with emotion but she reluctantly nodded, taking a step back. With his wife safely out of the way, he slid the key into the lock as quietly as humanly possible, not wanting to alert their visitor to his presence. When he turned the key, the lock was going to click and he had to assume that the intruder would hear it. All hell was about to break loose.

Sweat pooling on the back of his neck and the blood rushing in his ears, Tanner debated whether to turn the key slowly or quickly. Which would make the least amount of noise?

Quickly, he decided. Better to get it over with. Then go in and take down. That was the plan. Whether it was a good one or not? That remained to be seen.

I am getting too old for this shit.

Just wait until Logan or Jared or even Dare get to be my age. I'll bet they'll whine like little girls.

Turning the key to the right, the lock clicked, sounding incredibly loud in the silence. He pushed the door open but didn't see anyone right away but then a figure ran out from behind the couch, heading straight for the outdoor patio only a few steps away. They'd closed the door before they left and locked it but that didn't slow the intruder down much. He had it unlocked and slid open before Tanner could stop him.

Is he going to jump? He'll kill himself.

His fingers closed around the brass vase, tossing the flowers onto the floor. It had been too fucking long since he'd been the star quarterback of the high school football team, but some things a guy never forgets. He threw the vase at the intruder, the object zipping through the air and banging the guy on the temple, sending him staggering for a moment before righting himself and throwing a leg over the railing.

It appeared that he was going to try and climb down. Tanner wanted to be on the ground to meet him. Rushing back out the door he yelled at Maddie to call Ken Smith before shooting down the stairwell. Four fucking flights.

I am getting too old for this shit.

When he made it to the bottom his knees were screaming and he was sucking wind. Damn, he needed to make sure he worked out more regularly. He'd been slacking lately and it showed.

He rounded the corner of the building to the beach side but whomever had been in their condo was nowhere in sight. There were a few families enjoying the sunshine, some seagulls, and a jogger with big earphones but not their visitor.

What in the ever-loving fuck? Where had he gone?

Better yet, what had he been looking for?

Once again, a hell of a lot of questions and few answers.

What if I hadn't been here? What if Maddie had been alone?

He didn't want to think about that. Because if this guy laid one hand on Maddie, he'd wish he'd never been born.

Tanner was not a happy camper. He'd stomped around the condo for a few minutes and Maddie had simply let him work through his anger and frustration. He was mad because he was picturing her lying on the floor in a pool of blood. At this moment, it didn't matter that she wasn't dead or injured. He was thinking about the worst possible scenario and she knew better than to try and stop him. He had to work through this himself.

For the most part, he was calm and in control, but every now and then when he thought he couldn't protect someone he loved he went a little overboard. It wouldn't last long.

"You could have been here alone," he snarled, scraping his fingers through his hair. "Completely defenseless."

"That's true," Maddie replied, grabbing two waters from the refrigerator and handing one to him. He could use the help cooling off. "I don't have a tight spiral throw like you do. Aren't you glad you gave in and let me go with you to talk to Dina Wallace?"

He shot her a glare and proceeded to check out every nook and cranny of the condo.

"Did they get anything?"

"Doesn't look like it. I know they didn't get anything pertaining to the investigation."

He was finally calming down and now he was wearing a small smile.

"Because you hid it? Where?"

Their would-be burglar had opened every cabinet, drawer, and closet. He'd even rifled through the couch cushions and behind framed pictures.

"There was nothing to hide. All the files are electronic and on my phone."

"Smart. And that was never out of your sight."

Tanner patted his pocket. "They'd have to wrestle me for it."

"So did you get a look at the intruder?"

Grimacing, he shook his head. "Tall. Pretty big. From the looks, I think male. He was wearing dark slacks and shirt, plus a knitted cap over his face."

"Kind of hot for Florida."

"True, but I don't think he thought he was ever going to be outside. He flipped that lock on the patio door fast. I mean really, really fast. He had to have known where it was located. There was no hesitation on his part."

Unlike most doors, the lock on the patio wasn't at eye or chest level. It was down near the floor.

"So you think it was Leo?"

"I don't know. But…no. I don't think it was Leo. The guy was tall. Bigger than Leo, although he has the money to hire someone to do his dirty deeds. He wouldn't have to break and enter himself."

"You think he has henchmen?"

"Stranger things have happened. If he's a guy that's willing to kill his wife, he might also be willing to do other unlawful acts. But either way, he has a vested interest in making sure he doesn't go to jail. They may have been here to look for files or papers about the investigation or they may have been here to scare us."

"So what happens now?"

Funny, but she didn't feel scared. Tanner wasn't going to let anything happen to her. He'd be extra cautious from now on.

"We eat our food, watch the security camera footage, and go back to square one. Somewhere is a clue we've missed. We need to reconstruct it all and see what we come up with."

"Together?"

"Absolutely. You're not going to be alone anymore. Not until this killer is caught."

It wasn't the second honeymoon she'd planned but it sounded just fine.

CHAPTER TWENTY-TWO

They'd reheated dinner after Sheriff Ken Smith and his deputy left. The two men had taken a report about the break-in and they wholeheartedly agreed with Tanner.

The intruder wasn't looking for sunscreen. This was about the murder investigation.

Ken had profusely apologized about dragging Tanner into what might be a dangerous mess. The younger man didn't have enough experience to know that looking into a murder usually bothered the killer. Sometimes that meant they acted out. Sometimes it also meant that their actions brought about a break in the case. In this instance, Ken was going to speak to Brad about cameras in the elevators and stairwells. Their visitor might just have been caught on tape.

In the meantime, Tanner and Maddie had other video footage to comb through, which they did after eating and cleaning up the kitchen. Both of them curled up on the couch and Maddie had retrieved her tablet computer from her oversized handbag. There was film from three separate security cameras along the beach, plus the parking gate.

"It's harder to commit a crime these days," Maddie observed

as the first footage loaded. "There are eyes everywhere."

"That's very true," Tanner replied, cueing up the first clip. "Most people don't realize just how prevalent cameras are but they're almost everywhere now. If you walk down a sidewalk in a random neighborhood, chances are you're going to get picked up by someone's doorbell camera. Add in security cameras in traffic and business, and there's usually someone watching what you do at all times. Hell, even in Springwood we have red light cameras and I know for a fact that most of the store owners have them. Because I encouraged it. Video can close a case fast."

"I'm not sure how I feel about that. The thought that cameras are watching me is sort of disturbing. Add in how when I visit a website, ads for it follow me all over the internet and it's all kinds of creepy."

Tanner wouldn't argue with her.

"It's all creepy. I guess I'm old enough to be nostalgic for the good old days, but I do admit that being able to have movie showtimes and the weather at my fingertips is pretty cool. It's a give and take. Amanda won't know any different."

There were times when Tanner wanted his daughter to have the kind of upbringing that he'd had, but then he'd remind himself that the world was different now. She wasn't him. She'd have her own memories of childhood and hopefully she'd look back on them with happiness.

"The good old days," Maddie said with a chuckle. "My dad always said that the good old days weren't as good as we thought they were. That our memories were selective."

"Your dad is a wise man. Are you ready?"

The first video was taken from a security camera on the back door of the building next door. There wasn't much to see and it was quite dark. When two figures did appear, they were a distance from the camera and identifying them was impossible.

"Do you think that's Bibi?" Maddie asked, squinting to pick out any details. Tanner had zoomed in as far as he could but they were simply two dark figures.

"It could be. I could also be a million other people. The film quality is terrible." He sighed and cued up the next video. "Maybe the next will be better."

The second was from a security camera at a private residence. The quality was better and the footage wasn't nearly as dark. This time they could see a cat running across the sand and then a few minutes later two people walking by. One taller than the other. At first, Tanner didn't recognize them but then Bibi's scarf waved in the wind and she turned toward the camera for just a moment and he could make out her features. The person she was with, however, kept their back to the camera. Coincidence? Perhaps. Tanner couldn't identify Bibi's companion but he or she was taller and heavier.

The third video was worse than the first, at completely the wrong angle to show anything worthwhile. The fourth was from the guard house at the parking gate. The entrance was automated for residents between nine in the evening and six in the morning. There were plenty of comings and goings but none of them were Bibi, Leo, Randy, or Carrie.

"That was kind of a letdown," Maddie sighed. "I guess I was hoping for more."

"So was I," Tanner admitted. "It looks like we're not going to get lucky on this case. We'll have to find another way."

"If Logan was here, you'd ask him what his gut was saying."

She was right. He would have. Logan's gut was rarely wrong.

"What is your gut telling you?" Maddie asked. "Your instincts are usually just as right as Logan's."

Gut-check time. What was his intuition telling him?

"I can't prove it," he finally said, frustration in his tone. This case wasn't supposed to be this difficult.

"But?"

"I think Leo killed his wife. I know I shouldn't judge based on prior acts but the fact that this is his second wife dying young…"

They were both quiet, the only sound the low hum of voices from the television in the corner. He didn't know what Maddie was thinking about, but he was thinking that he needed to start at the beginning again. Go back to square one and see if he missed anything. Leo Gordon was leaving Florida soon. He didn't have much time if he was going to help Ken Smith.

"I'm going to stay up awhile, honey. Go through the investigation piece by piece again. I want to map out the relationships and the means, motive, and opportunity for each suspect. Logan's supposed to have more background information on Leo and Randy coming as well. I think I'll wait up for it."

"Then I think I'll head to bed. I'll leave my tablet out here for you." She pressed a soft kiss to his cheek and then stood. "I know better than to tell you not to stay up too late. Should I put on the coffee for you?"

His wife was the most understanding woman in the world.

"Nah, I've got it. Sweet dreams, babe. I'll come to bed when I finish here."

They both didn't believe a word out of his mouth.

What had he missed?

The next morning, Maddie woke just as the sun was peeking over the horizon. Reaching across the mattress, she laid her palm against the cool sheets on Tanner's side of the bed. He'd been up for a long time.

Assuming he'd ever come to bed to begin with.

Her guess was the latter. Tanner had worked some crazy hours over the years – and frankly so had she – and she'd learned not to stir too much if he came to bed in the middle of the night but she hadn't heard a single noise.

I slept too peacefully.

Throwing on a pair of yoga pants, she padded out into the living room on her bare feet and immediately spied her husband, sitting up but sort of sprawled out, his feet propped on the coffee table and the tablet computer on his lap. Dead asleep and softly snoring. His features were softer and more boyish in repose, and he looked so peaceful she was loath to disturb him. Her heart ached a little in her chest as she studied her husband.

I love this man.

Tiptoeing close to him, Maddie retrieved the tablet and then tucked the throw around him, stopping to brush a stray lock of silky hair from his forehead. He was devilishly handsome, far sexier than when they'd met. It really wasn't fair how men seemed to get more handsome as they aged. Or maybe she just loved him that much more.

He was asleep now, but he'd wake up soon when he smelled fresh coffee. As quietly as possible, she started the dark brew in the coffeemaker and then sat down at the small patio table to wait for it to finish.

Firing up the tablet, she could see that Logan had indeed sent some files in the early morning hours but Tanner must have already been asleep. The email hadn't yet been opened. She had a few minutes to kill until the coffee would be finished so she opened the files, the documents loading one by one.

Scrolling through each, she didn't see anything that stood out. Leo had come from a family with money, had married even more money, and was now loaded thanks to decent investments and a successful business.

Randy had come from a regular middle-class family but had managed to find his fortune playing professional football. He'd started his business – a string of pizza parlors – soon after retirement and although it had had its ups and downs, it had been mostly successful thanks to a few infusions of cash. The most recent from Leo Gordon.

She was head down over the files when a shadow fell over the table.

"I fell asleep."

Tanner was scraping his fingers through his hair, making it stand on end even more than it had been before. He looked like a sleepy little boy and her stomach clenched in her abdomen for a moment, reminding her of how Amanda looked in the morning. She wore that same half-scowl for the first five minutes of her day no matter how much sleep she'd had the night before.

"I can see that. How's your neck? You weren't in the most comfortable position for a good night's sleep."

Shifting his neck from side to side and wriggling his shoulders, he grunted and then sighed.

"I probably just should have come to bed when I got tired."

In other words, his neck and shoulders hurt. Probably his lower back too, but he'd never admit it in a million years.

"Logan sent those files early this morning. I've been looking through them while I waited for the coffee to brew. Can I pour you a cup?"

Tanner sat down heavily into the chair opposite. "It was the smell that woke me up. I can't believe I slept through you making coffee. Clearly I'm getting old and my hearing is going."

"You were tired and I was very quiet." She slid the tablet across to him. "Like a ninja."

He must have found the statement funny because he was

chuckling as she poured two cups of coffee. The smell was delicious and it woke her up a little bit more without even having to take a sip.

"What's my ninja-wife going to do about Gordon leaving? I haven't solved Bibi's murder and he's going to get on a plane and head for New York City, and then possibly leave the country if he's smart."

"I've been thinking about that. He may not leave the country. He might stay here. After all, he thinks he got away with it. Twice. He must be feeling pretty confident right about now."

"Maybe," Tanner grimaced, taking a sip of his lava hot coffee. "I think he did it, Maddie, but I can't prove it."

She could hear the frustration in her husband's voice. She'd been the one that had encouraged him to help Ken Smith and now the number one suspect was planning on getting on a plane and flying away.

"Why don't you let me fix breakfast this morning? And before you say anything, I think I can rustle up some scrambled eggs. They won't be as fluffy as yours but they will be edible. I haven't poisoned anyone yet and it's been months since we had to throw burnt food away."

Tanner really wanted to argue with her but apparently, he wanted to look at the information that Logan had sent even more.

My cooking is improving.

I can make eggs and toast, for heaven's sake.

Despite Tanner's dubious expression, he nodded in agreement, his head bent over the tablet while she cooked up the eggs. Carefully. She didn't want to give him any more reasons to think she was a lousy cook. There would be no throwing food in the trash this morning.

The toast was a no-brainer so it was with a little rush of

triumph that she placed two plates of eggs and toast on the table, along with two glasses and a jug of cranberry juice. They both preferred it to orange. She'd also placed the usual bottle of hot sauce next to his plate. He loved that stuff on his eggs. She'd tried it once and it had burnt a hole in her tongue.

"Thanks, babe."

He looked up briefly and shot her a grateful smile before pouring the sauce over his eggs and digging in. Maddie shuddered slightly as he took a huge forkful but she was also just so damn happy that the eggs had turned out so well. She'd surveyed the batch and there wasn't an eggshell in sight.

Go me.

"Are you going to call Logan–"

She didn't get the entire question out before Tanner had shot out of his chair, practically vibrating on his feet. For a moment she thought he was going to run to the sink to puke up breakfast but then she saw a smile cross her husband's face. She knew it well.

"What did you find?"

Tanner waved the tablet in the air, tapping the screen. She was so excited she didn't even care about the fingerprints. "Leo and Randy grew up in the same town, went to the same high school, although Leo was a few years ahead. Randy's dad worked for the company that Leo's dad owned."

"I'm not a cop. You're going to have to bottom-line it for me."

"This places Randy in Leo's life all the way back before his first wife Caroline died. Don't you see?"

Not really, but she wanted to.

"You think Randy killed Leo's first wife? And Bibi, too?"

She was trying to wrap her mind around it but her brain was telling her there were still too many unanswered questions.

"I think somehow Randy and Leo have been working together. I think that they're both involved in this. It's too much of
a coincidence. Randy had to know that Leo's first wife died but
he never mentioned it at all. Don't you think that's strange?"

Yes, she did. That was weird and if she had been in Randy's
place, she would have had a hell of a lot of suspicions about her
friend.

"Carrie was super upset when you questioned Randy," Maddie added. "Maybe she knows something as well. Could they all
be working together?"

If so, Bibi never had a chance.

"I don't know about Carrie. She could just be freaked out
that I was questioning her husband. I looked at the info that
Logan sent me on her and there isn't anything that stands out.
She could have her own suspicions."

The knock on the door interrupted their conjecture. They
weren't expecting anyone, especially at this hour.

Tanner took a peek out of the peephole. "It's Ken Smith."

The sheriff? He was out and about early this morning. Tanner opened the door and the sheriff strode in, waving his phone
in the air.

"We've got it," he crowed. "I was contacted by a homeown-
er who was out of town when the murder happened. They just
returned and were happy to send me their video from their
security camera. You'll never guess what it showed."

"Leo and Randy?"

Ken stopped, his brows pinched together. "Yes…how…did
you know that? Do you already have it? Shit, I thought I'd
broken the case wide open."

Tanner clapped the younger man on the shoulder. "You
have. It was just a lucky guess on my part. It turns out Leo and
Randy grew up in the same town and Randy's dad worked for

Leo's dad."

"Do you think they knew each other?" Ken asked. "That they were friends?"

"Maybe. I do think it's a coincidence that we need to check into further. Now let's see that video."

Ken cued it up on his phone. It wasn't a long clip but it showed Randy and Bibi walking on the beach. Fast forward about twenty minutes and Leo walked in front of the camera as well headed in the same direction. Was he going to meet Randy and Bibi?

"Is it enough to bring them in for questioning?"

"Absolutely," Tanner replied. "This is excellent work. Bring them in and question them about their past connections and also this video. Plus, you need to ask them about Leo's cash infusion into Randy's business."

"You mean you're going to ask them," the young sheriff corrected. "I wouldn't know what to do."

"Never a better opportunity to learn. How about we do it together?" Tanner suggested with a grin. "Now let's find Leo before he leaves Florida. We don't have much time."

This might finally be the break that they'd been waiting for.

CHAPTER TWENTY-THREE

Within the hour they were all crammed into the conference room at the sheriff's station.

Tanner, Ken, Randy, Carrie, and Maddie. It hadn't been Tanner's idea to have Carrie there but she refused to leave Randy alone with them. In fact, she'd been rather aggressive about the whole thing, calling cops in general a nasty name, and Tanner and Ken in particular a *really* nasty name.

Maddie had stayed to try and calm Carrie down and it had worked to a certain extent. Both women were sitting at the far end of the table while the three men sat at the other end. Randy had waived his right to a lawyer but not his wife, so she would stay for the time being.

First things first.

"Do you know where Leo Gordon is?" Tanner asked.

He couldn't be found anywhere. His luggage was still in his condo and his car was still in its parking space. But Leo? Missing. Ashley Monroe hadn't been found, either.

Looking nervous, his gaze darting all around the shabby room, Randy shook his head.

"No, I have no idea. He should be at home packing for New

York."

Ken snorted and hopped up from his chair. "If you're lying—"

Easy, buddy. We're just getting started.

"I'm not lying," Randy protested, his hands thrown in the air dramatically. "Why would I do that?"

That was Tanner's cue.

"That's an excellent question. Why would you do that? Why cover for a guy like Gordon?"

"Leo is a good guy. He's my friend."

"Who has had an extraordinary run of bad luck with wives," Tanner countered. "Bibi was the second to die young. His first wife Caroline was only twenty-five."

Randy's face went pale and his shoulders hunched slightly. The guy probably shouldn't take up poker.

"I don't know anything about that."

"Are you sure?" Tanner pressed, sliding a piece of paper in front of Randy. "Because we did some digging into your pasts and it turns out that you and Leo come from the same small town. Add to that, your dad worked for his dad. So let's ask a new question. How long have you known Leo Gordon?"

"Not that long. I didn't really know him back then."

"It's all just a crazy coincidence? You and Leo moving in the same condo building. Leo giving you money for your business."

A vibration in his pocket pulled Tanner away from the interrogation. He didn't like cell phones much and because of that no one would contact him unless it was important. With a quick apology, he checked his phone and saw a text from Logan. It was short and to the point. It was also going to be extremely helpful for this conversation.

"Sorry about that," he apologized again. "Now let's get back to coincidences. You're saying that all of this is just a weird coincidence. Is that correct?"

With a glance at his wife, Randy seemed to have re-centered himself and recovered his confidence. "That's correct. It's a small world. What can I say?"

"So you're going to tell me that it was a different Randy Knight that was Leo Gordon's alibi for his first wife's suspicious death?"

"I–Well–I–"

Ken's mouth opened but Tanner shook his head. Knight needed to figure this out himself without their help. This information was what Logan had texted him about. Randy Knight had been Leo Gordon's alibi all those years ago. He was the friend that Leo had been hanging out and drinking with.

Whatever bravado Randy had gained only moments ago had completely drained away. The man's gaze was down, his shoulders hunched. Tanner didn't prompt him in any way, content to let him figure out what he was going to say next. There was a long time with no one speaking and then finally he raised his head, his face a pasty color.

"It's not what you think."

"That's great. Tell me how it's different, because from where I'm sitting it looks like you and Leo conspired to kill his first wife and then again a few days ago." Tanner had cued up the video on his phone before coming into the conference room. "You're going to want to see this video from a security camera. You and Leo really should have been more careful. You were both captured on tape. You and Bibi walking down the beach and Leo following a while later. That's what cops call evidence, Randy. You're at the very least a person of interest in this case."

Carrie was openly crying now and Maddie was handing her tissues and patting her arm to calm her down. Randy watched the video, his eyes bright with tears.

"Let me tell you how this works where I come from," Tanner said. "I don't know if it works the same here but in my neck of the woods the first guy that starts talking gets the better deal. It can be you or it can be Gordon. Law enforcement really doesn't care much either way. They'll treat you as equals in these crimes even if it wasn't your idea."

"I didn't kill anyone."

Randy's voice was choked, his breathing ragged. He'd aged about ten years in the last five minutes.

"Do you want to tell me about it? Because if Gordon gets in here, he might not be so nice to you and keep his mouth shut. He might tell us his truth before we hear yours. Right now, we have you with Bibi right before she was murdered. Leo isn't on camera until later. He might say that he was covering for you."

Randy's eyes went round and he vehemently shook his head. "I didn't kill anyone. I swear. I would never do that."

Tanner held up the cell phone again. "You were seen walking down the beach with Bibi during the estimated time of death. Were you and Bibi having an affair?"

More sobs from Carrie but Tanner didn't let his gaze waver from Randy.

"No. No way. Uh-uh. Bibi and I were only friends."

"Then why were you walking with her in the middle of the night on the beach? I don't usually do that with friends. These are questions that a prosecutor is going to ask and a jury is going to think about."

Ken looked like he might explode but to his credit he didn't say a word. The tension built as Tanner waited...

Just a moment more...

Be patient...

Almost...

"Leo asked me to get Bibi out of the penthouse." Randy jumped from his chair, his hands holding each side of his head as if it might shatter into a million pieces. "It was all Leo's idea. It wasn't mine, I swear."

There it was. The beginning. People hated silence and eventually would try to fill it.

"In exchange for investing cash into your pizza business," Tanner said. "Do I have that right?"

"It's not like that. Leo gave me that money because we're friends."

Tanner and Ken exchanged a glance. The younger man looked shell shocked.

"And friends do things for each other, right?" Tanner replied. "Is that what Leo told you? This time and all those years ago with Caroline?"

Leaning his hands against the windowsill, Randy's head hung down. "He just asked me to tell the cops that he was with me. I didn't think it was a big deal. Caroline's death was an accident."

"Was it? Maybe. Did you wonder about it though when Leo asked you to lure Bibi out to the condo and then she turned up dead? Did it cross your mind about Caroline?"

Burying his face in his hands, Randy groaned. "I didn't know what he was going to do."

"What did you think he was going to do?"

Randy turned around, his eyes dark with emotion. "He said he wanted to tell her he was filing for divorce."

"On the beach?"

"He thought it would be neutral territory."

"At midnight? He wanted you to get Bibi out to the beach at midnight so he could tell her he wanted a divorce."

"That's what he told me. He told me to take her to one of my investment units and he'd tell her there."

If Logan had told Tanner that lame-ass reason, he would have kicked his best friend in the ass.

"Did you witness Leo strangling Bibi?"

There was a collective holding of breath as they all waited for Randy's answer. Even Carrie, who had been openly sobbing, seemed to quiet down to hear his reply.

"Ye–Yes. When Leo showed up, Bibi started in on him right away, yelling that he was a cheating scum and a bunch of other names. Leo grabbed her by the shoulders and told her to shut up, but she wouldn't. She kept yelling at him. At some point, he wrapped her scarf around her throat and…"

Randy's voice trailed away, clearly not wanting to say the word *murder*.

"Leo killed his wife? Is that your statement?"

"Yes," he sighed, his tone full of defeat. "That's my statement. It all happened so fast. One minute they were screaming at each other and the next he had her scarf wrapped around her neck. But I don't think he planned to do it. He was really upset afterward."

"What happened after that?"

"I panicked. I mean…shit…Leo had just killed Bibi. I said that we should call 911 and maybe they could revive her but Leo said it was too late. That we needed to make it look like a robbery or something."

Or something. That's what it had mostly looked like.

"Did you help Leo dump the body on the beach?"

Randy nodded, slumping back down into the chair. He appeared spent by his confession, sweat trickling down his forehead.

"Were you the one that broke into my condo yesterday? Did Leo ask you to do that?"

Leo didn't answer, his head hung down.

"He just wanted me to scare you a little bit. He wanted you to back off and leave the case alone."

It had only made Tanner more determined but then a man like Leo wouldn't understand that.

"Where is Leo? We can't find him."

Randy didn't answer again but Carrie abruptly stood, pushing her chair back so that the legs scraped against the dingy tile floor. Her makeup was a mess from her tears and she scrubbed at her cheeks with the back of her hand, making it worse.

"I'll tell you where Leo is. He's off to the airport. He dumped his bags at the penthouse and took a cab. He's not going to New York City. He's heading to the Cayman Islands. If you hurry, you might catch him."

She named the airline he was booked on and then her gaze swung to her husband.

"Bibi was my friend. I'll never forgive you for this."

Tanner turned to Ken, who had yet to comment on Randy's confession. "You ready to make your arrest, Sheriff?"

With a little luck, they just might make it before Leo Gordon's plane took off.

Maddie was still sitting with Carrie at the sheriff's station when Leo Gordon was brought in by two highway patrolmen. Randy was in the conference room giving a videotaped statement and Carrie had been inconsolable since he'd confessed to helping Leo lure Bibi out to the beach and also giving him an alibi for his first wife's death.

While Ken was taking Randy's statement, Tanner had been on the phone with Logan giving him an update as to what had happened. Maddie had assumed that Ken and Tanner would jump into a squad car and chase Leo down but they'd instead called the highway patrol and TSA.

Despite being handcuffed, Leo appeared confident, cool,

and unruffled when he was marched into the station. He stopped in front of Carrie and Maddie, giving the two women a big smile.

"It will all be fine, Carrie. Don't worry about anything. They have all of this wrong. I've already called my attorney and he'll be here any minute. I promise you Randy will be home soon."

Carrie vibrated with anger, her body visibly trembling. Maddie wrapped an arm around the older woman's shoulder to try and keep her calm. She was afraid that Carrie might lunge at Gordon if she didn't.

"Don't you dare speak to me," Carrie hissed at the smiling man, her fingers tightly clenching a ragged tissue. "You dragged Randy into all of this and now he'll spend the rest of his life in prison. And how could you do that to Bibi? She actually loved you. For real. If you didn't want to be with her you could have just filed for divorce, but you had to have everything your way, didn't you? You're a pathetic liar and I don't ever want you to speak to me again."

"No one is going to prison," Leo insisted. "This is all just a big misunderstanding. You'll see."

The door of the conference room swung open and Randy came out followed by Ken. Randy's eyes were red and swollen and honestly the sheriff didn't look much better. He was pale and sweaty, his hair askew as if he'd scraped his fingers through it one too many times.

"I told them everything."

Randy's voice was quiet but sounded booming in the silent hallway. Maddie watched Gordon's expression closely, but he didn't flinch or even bat an eyelash at his friend's declaration. He looked as if he didn't have a care in the world.

"Told them what?" Gordon asked. "There's nothing to tell because we didn't do anything illegal. This is all a misunderstanding perpetrated by an overzealous retired cop who has a God complex. Just because he caught one serial killer doesn't mean that everyone is a murderer."

It took a second for Maddie to figure out that Leo was talking about Tanner. A God complex? She couldn't think of anyone who fit that description less than her husband.

Tanner ended his call but ignored Leo, instead turning his attention to the sheriff.

"Your deputy Brian needs to speak with you right away."

Ken nodded. "I'll go talk to him. I'll be right back."

The sheriff hurried into the main station, leaving Randy and Leo in the hallway staring each other down. It was awkwardly quiet again but it might just be for the best. Maddie couldn't imagine that anyone had anything constructive to say at a moment like this.

"I'm sorry, honey. I'm so very sorry."

To Maddie's surprise, Randy's apology didn't send Carrie into another fit of sobs. Perhaps the poor woman was simply cried out. She blew her nose and then stepped forward, standing right in front of her cuffed husband.

"Sorry doesn't bring Bibi and that other woman back. Sorry doesn't repair my trust. Sorry isn't going to fix this. You're not the man that I've thought you were all of these years. It was all a lie and I was just the dumb wife by your side—"

Randy was shaking his head, a few tears spilling down his cheeks. "No, no, no. It wasn't like that. It was…it was stupid and I was stupid. We needed the money and I didn't have anywhere else to get it. Otherwise we were going to be bankrupt. Don't you see?"

Her countenance stony, Carrie stood her ground. "I see a man who would rather help take a life than to admit to his own business failures. I would rather have every material thing taken from me than to do what you've done. You're a coward, Randy Knight, and just looking at you makes me sick."

It was Randy's turn to break down into sobs but this time Carrie only watched impassively. At least for now, she was done crying. She'd have to be strong and Maddie didn't envy what the woman had ahead of her.

Ken strode back into the hallway, stopping to address Tanner. "The warrants were served to search Gordon's home and place of business. We found what we believe are Bibi Gordon's wedding rings and her diamond tennis bracelet in Leo Gordon's desk."

For a split second, Leo's mask of nonchalance slipped, revealing apprehension and more than a small amount of anger before he hid it once more.

"Looks like you've got this," Tanner said. "I'm going to take Maddie home. We still have a few days of vacation left."

Reaching out, Tanner slipped his hand into hers and led her down the hall and out into the Florida heat. He was right, they did still have some time left on their vacation but she couldn't imagine seeing Carrie, Ashley, or even Randy or Leo should they get out on bail.

"We're going back to the condo?" she asked after he helped her into the passenger seat of their rental car. "And then what?"

"I'm been thinking about that." He pulled smoothly out of the parking lot. "How about we pack up our stuff tonight and head to New Orleans? Let's get a hotel room and not talk to anyone else at all. Completely mind our own business. I can change our plane tickets."

The Big Easy? Hell, yes.

"I think that sounds like a great plan. Beignets and keeping to ourselves. We vow to speak to no one." She reached over and rested her hand on her husband's muscular thigh. "If you play your cards right, we never have to leave the room."

Let's get out of here.

"I'll hold you to that."

"I'm counting on it."

New Orleans sounded like a terrific place to learn to live life to the fullest.

Chapter Twenty-Four

It was almost time to go home to Springwood. Maddie and Tanner had enjoyed their time in New Orleans but they had a flight out first thing in the morning. It would be good to hug and kiss Amanda, sleep in their own bed, and get back into their regular routine.

A routine with one important difference.

Maddie was all about making every second count. Living life and savoring each moment she'd been given. She was a lucky woman and in a way that made her vulnerable because she had so much to lose. But if she lived her life scared then she'd be wasting all of these amazing gifts.

In a little shop just off of Bourbon Street on her first day in the city, Maddie had found a beautiful little notebook – the cover a riot of colors and the pages a sedate cream. Something had urged her to purchase it and since then she'd taken to writing down each morning at least one thing she was grateful for. It put her in the perfect frame of mind for the day, so she intended to keep it up once they were back home. She'd also started a kind-of bucket list. If she was going to live each day then there were a few items she wanted to tick off her to-do list.

It wasn't anything crazy like climbing Mount Everest or racing at Le Mans, but there were a couple of things she wanted to do. She wasn't completely boring, after all.

She and Tanner were sitting outside at a little cafe, the sound of jazz playing from inside. It was a warm and sultry evening in The Big Easy and the weather change was going to be a shock tomorrow. Right now, she was in a light sundress, sandals on her feet. By dinnertime tomorrow she'd be in sweaters and heavy socks.

"This has been a wonderful vacation," she said, sipping at her coffee. The entrees had been whisked away, leaving a decadent chocolate cake for dessert that they'd both shared. "Not bad for one that started with a murder."

"It's our own fault. We were friendly to strangers," Tanner replied with an almost straight face. "That never goes well."

She'd been thinking about their time in Florida…

"Did I force you to work on the case?"

His brow quirked and his smile widened. "Feeling guilty?"

"A little," she admitted. "I feel like I pressured you into helping Ken Smith when you really didn't want to."

"About that…I think that I was hesitating because I wasn't sure if helping on the case would make me miss my old job. Up until that moment, I'd surprised myself by not missing being sheriff. Sure, I still love a puzzle and solving a case but I don't miss the day to day grind, the paperwork. That's why I was pushing back on doing it. But I've found that I'm really okay with not being the sheriff anymore. I think…no…I definitely know that I'm going to run for mayor when we get home."

"You'll be the best mayor ever."

She meant that. He would do an amazing job.

"Let's not get crazy. There are things I need to learn about the job."

He underestimated himself.

"You know most of it because you've dealt with mayors throughout your career. Anything else I'm sure you can learn."

Laughing, Tanner pushed away the empty dessert plate. "Maybe this old dog will learn some new tricks."

"I'm rather fond of your old ones."

He leaned forward; his lips close to her ear. "If you're thinking what I'm thinking, let me pay the bill and we can get out of here."

Well…they did vow to keep to themselves.

"Ravish me, cowboy," Maddie whispered. "We've got one more night in The Big Easy. And I'm not playing hard to get."

Living life to the max.

Election Day…

Tanner couldn't believe all of the people that had come out to support his campaign for mayor. Not only local friends, but loved ones from miles away as well. His son Chris was there with his lovely girlfriend Ella, along with Logan Wright and his wife Ava. Jared and Jason sent their well wishes but unfortunately couldn't make it because of work. Dare Turner and his wife Rayne had also stopped by.

His daughter Emily was sick with the flu, but Tanner had spoken to her earlier in the day and she was sending out strong positive vibes for his win. Amanda was home asleep – cuddled with her new puppy Foster – and with a sitter, but she'd wished her daddy good luck and given him the thumbs up sign. She'd made him promise to wake her up if he won.

Everyone had gathered at the local sports bar as they awaited the voting results. There was a huge banner hanging from the ceiling that said "Tanner Marks – Springwood's next mayor." He was positive that Maddie was responsible for that. She'd taken to calling him mayor these last few weeks. That's how sure she was that he was going to win.

He wasn't as convinced.

Could it be this easy? Hopping from one career to another? A few months ago, he would have told anyone that suggested he run crazy but here he was, hoping to win an election. The last election he'd won was captain of the football team in high school, and that was a damn long time ago.

Maddie kept telling him that he was extremely popular in Springwood and that every person she talked to was going to vote for him. But what if they were only saying that because they didn't want to seem rude and hurt her feelings? What if he lost...in a landslide?

"You look like you're about to lose your lunch."

Those sentiments came straight out of Logan's mouth. The ladies had gathered around a table waiting for the election results and the men had gathered near the bar and the televisions.

"It's a possibility," Tanner admitted, taking another gulp of his ice water. They'd ordered several appetizers but he was far too nervous to eat. "I could lose badly tonight."

Chris laughed and shook his head. "Are you being serious? You're a shoo-in to win. The straw poll over at the barbecue place has you way ahead. You're not going to lose. You're going to win, Dad."

"But if you do lose, you can always come work with me," Logan said, tongue in cheek. "Drown your sorrows in a cold case, for example."

Logan had taken the news that Tanner wasn't going to accept the job offer with his usual good grace, but that didn't stop him from busting his friend's balls every now and then.

"Dad's moved on and up," Chris said. "I think he's done

with law enforcement."

"When you do win, what's the first thing you're going to do as the new mayor?" Dare asked. "Run that old weasel of a mayor out of town?"

That had crossed Tanner's mind more than once. He was sure that not all of Pete's business dealings were on the up and up.

But he had more important items on his list. The very first...

"Hire Sam as the sheriff," Tanner replied. "And pay him what he's worth. In fact, pay all of the deputies and other first responders a decent wage. That's what I ran on and that's what I'm going to do."

"He'll do a great job," Chris said. "Maybe you could hire Ken Smith as a deputy. He might be ready to leave all of that Florida sunshine."

"Very funny, son. I doubt that Ken would ever want to move someplace where it gets below seventy degrees on a regular basis. I did talk to him a couple of days ago. He's decided not to run again for sheriff. He's going to look for a computer programming job. He says that law enforcement isn't for him."

"He's probably made the right decision," Dare said.

"I feel for him," Tanner replied. "He was thrown into the job with no training. I think he'd be okay if he had someone to guide him."

"Like Sam," Logan said with a grin. "He's good with young deputies."

"Like Sam," Tanner agreed. "He's a born leader. He'll be a great sheriff for Springwood."

He was happy to pass the baton. That was the way of life and it was time. He couldn't go on forever, and frankly, he didn't want to. He'd had a great career and accomplished so much but there were other ways to help his community.

"Did Smith say anything about the case against Leo Gordon and Randy Knight?" Logan asked, popping a cheese fry into his mouth.

"He did. The DNA from the skin under Bibi's fingernails belongs to Gordon. He, of course, is saying – or his lawyer is – that there's nothing unusual about a husband's skin under a wife's fingernails. Because of…you know…sex."

"He might win that argument," Dare said, his expression fierce, but then he was always in a state of general grouchiness. His wife even called him *grouchy bear*. The guys had never let him forget it, either. "I'm always shocked by the twisted logic of criminals. Sometimes they even get away with it."

"It's a possibility," Tanner agreed. "So far his strategy seems to be pointing the finger at Randy Knight. If they were friends before, they aren't now. They're each blaming the other. It just might work to put enough reasonable doubt into a jury. Leo is also insinuating that Ashley Monroe could be behind the murder. A woman scorned thing."

Ashley Monroe had eventually been found in Palm Springs staying with friends. She steadfastly maintained that she'd never argued with Bibi and that she wasn't having an affair with Leo. Tanner believed her. There was no evidence that she'd had anything to do with Bibi's death.

"I'm guessing that's their plan," Chris said. "They might still be friends and working together, if you know what I mean. I've seen crazier things."

Now that Tanner had some distance from the case, he was convinced that Leo had planned to kill Bibi that night. The story he'd given Randy about simply wanting to tell her about the divorce didn't hold water. It wouldn't be a stretch to think that Randy also knew what Leo had planned for his wife and was an active participant.

Chris's cell rang and he pulled it from his pocket. "It's Annie. I want to tell her goodnight. I'll be right back."

Tanner's son headed outside to get some quiet, leaving Tanner with Logan and Dare.

"So are you okay?" Logan asked, tossing a glance over his shoulder to be sure that Chris was out of earshot. "No more mid-life crisis?"

Dare's brows shot up. "You were having a mid-life crisis? Aren't you a little late for that?"

Shit, these guys would be the death of him.

"I'm planning on living a very long life," Tanner replied, sarcasm in his tone. "And I wasn't having a mid-life crisis, asshole. I was just in flux as to what direction to take my career."

"It sounds like a mid-life crisis to me," Logan said with his patented grin. "But I guess I could be wrong."

"You were wrong."

Logan didn't need to know that both Tanner and Maddie had been at crossroads in their lives. But they'd hiked through the rough patch and were firmly on the other side. He knew what he wanted and didn't want, and Maddie was living more in the moment than he'd ever seen her.

It was damn fun to watch, too. They were even putting together a joint bucket list. Things they wanted to do together, and as a family.

Dare rolled his eyes. "Can you imagine Logan having a mid-life crisis? He's already a major pain in the ass. He'd be completely intolerable."

"Fuck you," Logan replied with a smirk. "I am not intolerable. Just ask Ava."

"That poor woman," Dare lamented. "I can't imagine what she goes through on a daily basis putting up with you. She's a saint."

"All our wives are saints," Tanner corrected. "They're way too good for us, but luckily they don't see it that way."

Chuckling, Logan raised his longneck to his wife, who was deep in conversation with Ella.

"Speak for yourself. Ava tells me that she's a saint all the time."

Now that he was thinking about it, Tanner had heard Ava do just that on a few occasions. He did think that Logan was exaggerating about the *all the time*, though.

He felt a tug on his shirtsleeve and looked down to find Maddie at his elbow.

"Look on television," she urged. "The returns are in."

The bartender zoomed up the volume and the entire place seemed to get quiet almost immediately. The local news anchor was speaking, saying that the turnout for the election was record-breaking. The votes flashed onto the screen and Tanner had to concentrate to be able to comprehend what they meant. There was his name with a number and Pete's name with a number as well.

"You won," Maddie crowed, throwing her hands in the air and then around Tanner. "You won. You're the new mayor."

A roar swelled up from the crowd and a bewildered Tanner found himself the recipient of many handshakes, hugs, and slaps on the back. He kept craning his head to look at the television screen, which had turned the vote count into a news crawl at the bottom.

He'd won. By a landslide. It wasn't even close.

Tanner was the new mayor of Springwood.

"I'm so proud of you and I love you so much," Maddie whispered as she pulled him down for a kiss. "You're going to be the best mayor this town has ever seen, Tanner Marks."

He was going to try.

Logan lifted his bottle. "A toast to Tanner and his new job. Springwood is a lucky town. And when he's done here, it's on to the state legislature and then Washington."

A cheer went up from the crowd and Tanner shook his head to try and take it all in. Mayor? State legislature? Washington D.C.?

Well...why the hell not? Springwood wasn't the only place where people needed help. If this mayor thing worked out...

As long as he had the love of his life by his side anything was possible. His beautiful Maddie. She was a wonderful mother and wife. He loved her more each day and he was fucking glad that he'd been given a second chance at love with her. He'd never take it – or her – for granted.

Together they'd savor every moment.

Thank you for reading! I hope you enjoyed Bitter Justice. There will be more stories in the Cowboy Justice Association series. Coming soon.

Thank you again for reading.

About the Author

Olivia Jaymes is a wife, mother, lover of sexy romance and cozy mysteries, and caffeine addict. She lives with her husband, son, and two spoiled dogs in central Florida and spends her days typing on her computer with a canine on her lap.

She is currently working on a new cozy mystery series – *A Ravenmist Whodunit* – in addition to her other ongoing romance series.

Visit Olivia Jaymes at
www.OliviaJaymes.com